T0128941

SWIFT JUSTICE

JUSTICE

THE CLANDESTINE PROTECTORS

DEWAYNE RUCKER

authorHOUSE®

AuthorHouse™
1663 Liberty Drive
Bloomington, IN 47403
www.authorhouse.com
Phone: 833-262-8899

*This is a work of fiction. All of the characters, names, incidents, organizations, and dialogue
in this novel are either the products of the author's imagination or are used fictitiously.*

Published by AuthorHouse   06/17/2024

ISBN: 978-1-5462-2101-2 (sc)
ISBN: 978-1-5462-2100-5 (hc)
ISBN: 978-1-5462-2104-3 (e)

Library of Congress Control Number: 2017918978

Print information available on the last page.

*Any people depicted in stock imagery provided by Getty Images are models,
and such images are being used for illustrative purposes only.
Certain stock imagery © Getty Images.*

This book is printed on acid-free paper.

DEDICATION

This story is dedicated to the men and women who are serving and protecting the communities in which we live, and, for those who work behind the scenes supporting those who devote their lives protecting others.

ACKNOWLEDGEMENTS

A special thanks to my wife, Maureen, for her patience, support and continued encouragement for simply finishing my story. To the select family members who willingly assisted with the multiple edits, Maureen, Tehra, Roscoe, and Danielle, I sincerely thank you. Thanks, Don, for your editing suggestions and personally understanding author challenges. Thanks to my family, extended family, friends and readers for supporting my venture. My wish is that the words on these pages invoke thought as well as entertainment.

CHAPTER 1

Meg removed the magazine from the black handle of her GLOCK 27. Pulling back the slide ejected the one hollow point round from the chamber. She placed the one round with the fully loaded magazine in the wooden box before securely locking them and the weapon in her closet. The .40-caliber was not something any woman would choose for a personal protection handgun. Then again, Megan Emily Swift wasn't just any woman, and she didn't take too kindly to the stereotype. At age twenty-four, she fulfilled many of her dreams. She had few regrets. The one milestone in life, which seemed to escape her, wasn't on her bucket list. She knew very well the clock was ticking and had all but given up on a sustainable, rewarding relationship. Everywhere she looked and everything she read, led to the same life fulfillment: a house, a husband, two-and-one-half kids, and living comfortably on two incomes in the suburbs of a city. Megan was not--and never had been--the typical woman. She had grown up in a non-typical household. Her mother and father had saved for years to get her into a college of her choice. They knew early on their little girl was gifted. Their hopes and dreams for their daughter came with lots of hard work, sacrifice and many prayers. They wanted for her whatever she wanted for herself. They were the best parents Megan could have dreamed of having. Being an only child meant she didn't have to compete as hard as those children in two-and-one-half-kid families. Megan did well in high school--very well. Her brains got her into the flagship University of Missouri, MU; then ultimately, Missouri University School of Law. Although they wanted her to spread her own wings and find her niche, it appeared she too, would follow in her parents' footsteps by becoming

1

an attorney. Like any teen just out of high school, she had the world figured out. Her parents taught her to stand on her own two feet and think for herself. She was strong-willed, and it served her well. She never experienced the bullying like many kids did. It was never a question of why. She was tough--not just on the inside, but on the outside as well. She stood up for herself and for others who seemed to not find their own voice. Both of her parents were athletes, and Megan held up the family tradition. Although she could never dunk a basketball with just one hand, she could wrap fingers around the rim and box out any foe inside the paint who thought she was meager. She was a force to be reckoned with. She got her five-foot ten frame from both her parents. Her hazel eyes were mesmerizing. Women envied her shoulder length, naturally curly, brunette hair. It was the blonde highlights and athletic physique that caught the eye of both men and women. It was her athletic ability that got her noticed by all those who either read the sports page of the local paper or attended one of the school's games. Her athleticism didn't capture the attention of any Ivy League scouts, as the small southwest Missouri town never seemed to warrant any prospective sport heroes. She had grown up most of her life answering to the name of "Meg". Her name, shortened by her parents, stuck through high school, college, and her post graduate pursuit in Columbia. She liked her name, and her life was on track.

Then came one, memorable, warm, spring day. While in class, her professor got a message handed to him from his administrative assistant, Shirley McPherson. Unbeknownst to Meg, that message would change her life forever. The interruption came at a time when all ears hung on every syllable uttered from the professor's lips. The class of twenty-eight students was focused. Their attendance in class hadn't been mandatory. It wasn't on this day either; however, this professor had a reputation of "tell all" when it came to what's expected on exams. Finals were fast approaching, and Meg was on track for another stellar academic year. She was already being offered an internship at a prestigious law firm. Her fall semester looked promising, with one foot in the door for what hoped to be a rewarding law career. Not that passing the bar would be easy, but she was confident in her abilities; her professors had repeatedly rewarded her with praises of future accolades.

There was a noticeable pause in the class instruction, and all eyes were on the professor. Dr. Theodore "Ted" Morris had more letters of the alphabet behind his name than many of his colleagues. His knowledge of law, coupled with his wittiness, made his courses popular with students. He had been interrupted by his assistants before, so students were used to a few minor breaks in discussions. This one was different. Dr. Morris seemed taken back. He stared at the note as if it were in a different language.

He looked up at the class and uttered the words, "Excuse me."

His monotone was almost a whisper. If it weren't for the wireless microphone pinned to his shirt collar, the class would not have heard him. He turned and left the room. A hush came over the class. This was a first. Everyone was intent on his every word. Each student was mindfully aware their success depended on how they interpreted the instructed content for the upcoming final. Being absent in class during the year wasn't a death sentence, provided each written exam was thoughtfully and thoroughly completed. After a seemingly exhaustive delay, Dr. Morris reentered the room. He was noticeably shaken. It was as if a client had failed to tell him a critical point for a successful defense, and the prosecution was aware of the omission. He glanced up, looking directly at Meg. He then appeared to scan across the tiered rows of seating as if looking for an answer to a question from a specific student. But it was obvious. He had locked eyes way too long with Meg, and the class of brilliant observant minds also caught the glare. Meg's stomach fluttered as she, too, noticed the obvious.

"Sorry for the interruption class, where were we?"

He stumbled through his notes as if he wasn't prepared. He was always prepared.

"Analytical separation from the accused client's charge," Meg quipped with a nervous stutter.

She couldn't get past the lingered glance from Dr. Morris following his return to the classroom. She was caught off guard.

Meg sat on the second-row seat, center stage as she always did. It wasn't by accident that Dr. Morris knew where Meg sat. It was as if she was supposed to have known she would have been called upon to help bring back the previous awkwardness of the class interruption.

She could always be counted on to interject with an answer. Others did, as well, throughout the academic year as if it were a contest. Meg held her own, and classmates were consciously aware of how talented she was in grasping the subject matter. For her, it was like sitting home at the kitchen table bantering with her parents following a report on the evening news. There would be deep discussions of the guilt or innocence of someone arrested and charged with a serious crime.

Dr. Morris found his place, but he was off his game. He wasn't as sharp as he always seemed to be. He was no longer poised with perfection. It wasn't like him and the class was painfully aware. He glanced at the clock at the back of the room.

"Class dismissed; I'll see you all Monday."

Normally, class was held to the top of the hour, especially this close to finals. Out thirty minutes early was awarding college students to go enjoy the weekend early on a Friday. It was a Friday; and Meg was planning on taking in some of the three-game, SEC women's, softball tournament with Texas Tech. This was another sport in which Meg had found prowess. She liked the physical challenge of basketball, where she could show her strength and competitiveness.

"Meg Swift, please stop by my office before you leave today."

Dr. Morris' voice came clearly through the speaker system. He had always called her Meg. His inclusion of her last name made it seem official, far too official. The wrestling of notebooks and students gathering up their belongings seemed to hush, if only for a second. It seemed as if all eyes were on her, and they were. The complete class looked at her with wondering eyes. It was obvious--the note, the class delay, and interruption were all about her. This seemed urgent. No time for emails forwarded from instructors to students. This was personal.

CHAPTER 2

Megan sat in the plush, elegant office. The chair folded around her like a warm, gentle blanket. There was one problem, she couldn't get comfortable. It wasn't the seat; it was the occasion. How could she sit comfortably waiting for the unknown? She had been there previously for counseling visits regarding her progress, or lack of it. Other students in his class were asked to visit with him as well. This was the first time, however, that she had ever been invited into his office without him being there. Dr. Morris's assistant seemed distant. She hadn't been that way before, and Meg sensed it was intentional. Her eyes were averted; there was busy work, and her typing on the computer keyboard appeared intentional to avoid conversation. Her suggestion for Meg to enter Dr. Morris' office and to wait for him was a sign—and not a good one. It all seemed odd, although she tried to sit comfortably in the exquisite surroundings.

There were reasons for all things, and she was totally convinced of that. Her moral compass was rock solid, and people who were acquainted with her were comfortable with that fact. Nothing was comfortable about where she was, and she was anxious about Dr. Morris wanting to see her. Meg knew her grades were good, and she had hoped this upcoming final would sustain her perfect four-point standing.

She was almost startled when Dr. Morris rounded his desk to sit down. She hadn't heard him enter. Her mind was focused on the unknown. She gave him her familiar smile that would melt any person who was on the receiving end. It took years for Meg to realize she was beautiful. Megan knew of her inner beauty, but she was naïve to her other attributes.

It was, in part, those attributes that made what Dr. Morris had to tell her so difficult. It was because of her intellectual prowess that it was much harder. Her world was going to be turned upside down.

"I don't know how to tell you this, Meg. I got a call from the campus police this afternoon."

"Was that the note Shirley brought you?" Meg quickly responded. "I knew it had something to do with me. But let me explain, it wasn't me who put shaving cream on Stephen's car. I saw some of the guys before class today, and they were all laughing about it, and said the word was out that I did it. They were joking of course. My apartment is off campus, and I wouldn't drive to town and on campus just for a prank."

Meg's nervous smirk quickly turned neutral. She could tell he was serious and she was rambling.

"Meg, let me explain. Campus police called to say they were contacted by the Greene County Sheriff's Department."

"Sheriff Macintyre? I haven't seen him in years. How's he doing?"

Dr. Morris let Meg continue until she realized she was nervously babbling again. She paused to let him continue. Her nerves were causing a nauseous feeling, something she hadn't experienced in years. The last time was her senior year in high school during the championship basketball game. It was overtime, and the game was on the line.

"Meg, are you OK?" Dr. Morris noticed the blank stare in her eyes. She was staring at the shingles behind him on his wall. She was not herself, and he knew it was quickly going to get worse.

"Yes, Dr. Morris. I'm fine. You were saying you talked to Sheriff Macintyre."

"I talked with the campus police. It was they who spoke with the Greene County Sheriff's Department. Meg, I have some very bad news to tell you."

He watched Meg's face turn pale. He had never been given the task of telling a student news of this magnitude. He usually had sent warnings through email regarding their failing grades or missed assignment deadlines. It was during the counseling sessions he often recommended students change majors or perhaps withdraw from his courses. Some students didn't have the intellect to pursue their lofty dreams. It bothered him to inform them of those facts. Most students were relieved with the options they were presented. Their college careers would still be intact. He wasn't sure about Meg's after today.

"This is the most difficult thing I've ever had to do," the professor continued. He knew he couldn't mince words. He had to deliver the message in simple words.

"Earlier this afternoon, your mom and dad were both killed in a traffic accident."

He continued to explain what had been relayed to him as to what occurred. He knew she would want to know details of what happened. Before returning to the classroom from the unintended break, he had his administrative assistant compile the contact names and phone numbers of those who could possibly answer the questions he couldn't. He reached out to Meg, holding the information on a notepad only to place it on his desk. She hadn't heard much more of what he had told her.

Dr. Morris called for Shirley to come into his office. He had warned her of the probability Meg would need consoling. He was right. What person, as close to their parents as Meg had been, could hold it together after learning of their deaths? An illness is one thing, but a traffic accident resulting in untimely loss of life is incomprehensible.

He left his office allowing his assistant and Meg to be alone. It was heartbreaking. He could hear Meg sobbing uncontrollably in his office. It was not going to be a day soon forgotten, not by a long shot. After a short while, which seemed like hours, his assistant came from his office and quietly closed the door. She wanted to give Meg some time to be alone with her thoughts before leaving. Dr. Morris then began to wonder if the crying he heard was all Meg's. Shirley was obviously upset and had been crying as well. It was somber. No one spoke but just sat waiting for Meg to come out of Dr. Morris' office. It was almost as if the lingering moment had frozen in time.

The door slowly opened as if it was being pulled by a draft from an adjacent door or open window. She stepped out and slowly walked to the office entrance doorway before stopping when Dr. Morris called to her.

"Meg, is there anything I or my office can do for you?"

"It's 'Megan.' My name is 'Megan.' My mom and dad called me 'Meg;' my name is 'Megan.' I would appreciate you calling me by my name."

CHAPTER 3

It had been only a few months since that dreadful day when Megan's world was turned upside down. She'd come a long way from picking up the shattered pieces. She miraculously passed her final exams, although there wasn't a professor who thought there was a possibility otherwise. The stress of losing her parents and the wanting to not disappoint them caused a near emotional breakdown. Her extended family, whom she had never really known, immediately reached out to her. She realized, however, it was for financial gain rather than bloodline that brought them to her aid. Megan's parents had multiple life insurance policies in her name and her name only.

Unbeknownst to her, she was financially sound. Her parents made sure of that, although she had no idea until a visit from a family friend. Brian Finch, the bank loan officer, had been a friend of her parents for many years. He came by to pay his respects one week after the services – so she thought. Megan couldn't remember his name and barely recognized him at all. Why would she, he just worked at the bank? She had her debit card, and there were no faces attached to the plastic she carried. It was only a form of unlimited cash to her. He came to explain to her the beneficiary addendum to the life insurance policies. She would never have to work a day in her life. With that in mind, she was tormented with the thought of something happening to her. It became too much to handle. She found herself sinking deeper and deeper into a world she hadn't recognized before that dreadful spring day that seemed like so long ago.

Perhaps she shouldn't have gone to the scene of the accident. She had to know for herself and see why her world had changed forever. Her fragile state, compounded with not understanding the "why", left her near the brink of disaster. She learned exactly where and what happened on that lone four-lane road in rural Greene County, Missouri. Self-consciously, she knew she needed closure. Going to the scene of the crash would help with that. She learned a simple tire deflation caused her world to fall apart.

She had read about it in the newspaper and knew exactly how many miles from the small town of Republic the crash had occurred. Driving east on US 60 toward Springfield, she slowed her car to a near crawl and then pulled to the shoulder and stopped. The sun glared into her eyes, but she could still see the broken glass deep within the grass. She knew this was the place where it all had occurred. She had driven by it before not realizing what she had seen. Orange spray paint had then marked critical yaw striations where her parents' vehicle careened off the pavement. Only fifteen feet from the shoulder was the culvert, which caused it to overturn. Deep tire ruts were in the turf, and gouges into the soft clay left broken brake light and parking lens littering the right-of-way. There were what looked like plastic bumper parts and other debris. She could smell the oil and gasoline mixture that permeated the air. Cellophane packaging was strewn all over the ground. Other indescribable debris from the on-duty emergency medical crew were scattered about.

She heard EMS had done all they could to save her parents that afternoon. The crew had worked beside the fire department extricating her parents from their car. Grass was matted down from apparent footprints from the scores of people who were there. She could see blood-stained gauze bandaging amongst the other traffic crash carnage. She couldn't bear to think what the scene was like to have been there. She felt that uncontrollable nauseous feeling in the pit of her stomach again. There would be no roadside markers placed at this site, not by her; and she knew none of her parents' relatives would either. Roadside memorials were being placed all over Missouri's landscape as reminders to travelers of tragedies that had taken place at those sites. She didn't need a reminder. She had seen enough and would remember it long after all the evidence of its occurrence was gone. She never wanted to return to the site where her parents died and vowed not to. She had submitted all the information needed for a copy of the accident report from the Highway Patrol. That's all she wanted if she someday chose to recall it to memory. Once received, if she could bear to look at it, she would put it in a safe place.

The small community wrapped their arms around her, and she felt like she could make it her home forever. Besides, it was her home. She knew so many people, or so she thought. After all, she had been away for several years, only to return for visits with her parents. You never know just how true your friends are until tragedy strikes or hard times engulf you. She never had any real close friends in school. She just wanted to get out of high school and start her life. The warm caring visits from people slowly trickled to nonexistence. The phone calls expressing concern for her well-being ceased. She found herself sinking slowly into a depressed state. She declined the promising internship, realizing there was much to be done to get her life in order. The fall semester came and went. She ignored the written correspondence from Dr. Morris, but the phone messages continued. It was comforting to know her professor was interested in the fulfillment of her dreams of a law degree. She made a courtesy call to confirm her degree was on hold until some future date. She had a nice visit with Shirley, and thanked her for her kindness during such a difficult time. She hadn't realized until that conversation just how difficult it must have been for her as well. She could hear her voice crack and could visualize Shirley wanting to comfort her once again. Megan was all cried out. Shirley insisted she wait on the line until Dr. Morris completed his long-distance phone call. He had mentioned on several occasions wanting to speak with Megan if she reached out to his office. Megan extended greetings to the office and especially Dr. Morris. She expressed apologies for not calling sooner and asked Shirley to tell everyone "hello" for her. She said she was doing fine and hoped to visit them soon. Megan hung up the phone realizing her voice sounded full of cheer. She didn't want to sound like she often felt. Her focus was not on her law degree; it was on her mental health.

The call to Mizzou's School of Law brought back a flood of memories. All the good ones were overshadowed by one. Megan knew she had to shake the fog of feeling sorry for herself. It was time to fend off what it was that was dragging her down. Although she realized it was not in her complete grasp, she felt she was finally on the right path to recovery. She was finding strength and was at the proverbial fork in the road. She had lost her way and understandably so. There seemed to be no purpose. Her mental health was on frayed threads. She was trying to mend those threads but seeking professional help, to her, meant a personal failure. She had no one to tell her otherwise. She was finding her strength from her parents. She had listened to them before. Why hadn't she paid attention to what they were trying to tell her now? It was her physical strength that sustained her mind. Her body was fine-tuned. It had always been. She never faltered in her exercise. Megan did realize she was slowly finding her purpose. She would do her run in the early morning and hit the YMCA midafternoon. She forced herself to enter the gym realizing she would be recognized in the small town. People would once again want to console her, and she would revisit the torment from what seemed like a long time ago. It didn't happen. She saw people who came to see her, and promised to return, but never did. She noticed the awkward shyness or diverted eye contact. No one wanted to speak to her or were afraid of what they might say. She understood completely. She felt the same.

Taking control of her life hadn't been easy. It seemed like a long time before she realized she had to take control. She slowly convinced herself she had to do something positive. It was that purpose she was searching for; her confidence and resilience had waned. Her parents would have been disappointed in her loss of purpose and her pursuit of happiness. She knew they wouldn't have understood. Her mother would have given her that stern look of "what are you doing to yourself?" It would have lasted for as long as it took for her to understand the disapproval. Her father would have had the talk--his gentle way of getting her to understand his disapproval. His way was devastating. She always felt like he was yelling at the top of his lungs although he never raised his voice. The guilt trips always worked well with both parents. She was getting the message, but she hadn't reached the top of the rung and that glimmer of light seemed like it was forever snuffed out. She missed them dearly.

She would push her cardio training when she knew she needed it. She was fully aware of her mental well-being. Exercise was her way of being self-medicated. Her parents had taught her early on that a strong body made a strong mind. She never doubted their wisdom. There were times when she resisted their way of thinking, but this wasn't one of those. She hadn't managed to pull herself back to full strength mentally, and she was fully aware of it. Her lack of close intimacy and social life were the norm as well. She knew the stress brought on by finals and the pressure she put on herself. She wasn't ready to venture back into that.

Her escape to the Y was good for her, and she knew it. She was finding peace and was in search of purpose. She felt so alive when on her run or at the gym. It was comforting feeling good again. That glimmer flickered one mid-afternoon at the gym. She had pushed herself to the limit and then some. She extended her reps and increased the weight. She felt she needed it. She knew she needed it. She had been down this road before in her recovery, but she felt--no, she knew--she was at a turning point. She called it--recovery. She would sometimes run a little harder and a little longer during her morning routine. She was feeling alive again, and it felt good.

She finished her routine oblivious, as always, to her surroundings. Her focus was where it belonged, on her strength endurance. She threw a towel over her head to dab the sweat off her brow. She turned, backing away from the resistance machine.

"Oh, I'm sorry," she exclaimed stepping on one of his tennis shoes while rudely bumping into him. Her right shoulder struck him firmly in his sternum as she straightened while gaining her balance.

"You're fine," he said as he continued walking past her. To him, it was like it hadn't happened. He was good at what he did. He was always in tune with his surroundings. He had noticed her before and admired her. Not for her fitness, although it was a plus, but for her focus. Gyms had turned into social gatherings. If they didn't come there with someone, they wanted to leave with somebody. He noticed she never came with anyone and rarely conversed with others. Megan walked a safe distance after a brief few steps; then, she turned. He hadn't turned to look at her. He was already into his reps for his upper body routine.

Megan turned up the corners of her mouth in a smirk and thought to herself, "I'll pay more attention next time." She had noticed him during her workouts before and appreciated his focus. She liked the fact that he didn't seem to give her the time of day.

CHAPTER 4

Chad Jerguson had done his homework. He didn't like to make mistakes. He timed the cool down from his workout to watch her leave the gym. The gym was littered with equipment spaced comfortably throughout. He came to the gym at approximately the same time, three days a week. Midafternoon was precisely the preferred time. Not just for him, but for Megan as well. She was leaving with her bag draped over her shoulder. He wondered why she had her shoulder bag this time. She normally showered at the Y following her workouts. He watched her by peripheral vision from a safe distance across the facility as she walked out. She looked for him. It was obvious to him, as she had glanced toward the leg extension machine he was using when she left the facility. He had moved on from that, and she scanned the machines like an eagle searching for prey. She slowed her gait while walking and scanned the gym. Still looking for him.

Chad casually turned, glancing toward the foyer and an empty attendant's desk. He watched her as she glanced in his direction, finally locating him. She almost failed to engage the push bar on the door to allow her exit. He knew she glanced his way. She knew he had seen her walking out and was looking her way.

Megan smirked to herself, "Hmm, I may have to adjust my upper body routine schedule."

His workout was complete and he, too, was ready to leave. He would have shortened his exercise today anyway. His mission was accomplished. He made contact, and was a little surprised how it was received. He had made no effort before; he was a professional. He knew when it was right, and hadn't missed his mark. She wasn't ready until now, and he hoped he hadn't rushed it. He had watched her from a safe distance. He noticed her style, her focus, and when she wasn't focused. She had so many telling signs. He at one time became concerned for her safety. She seemed like she might not make it out of her slump. Her eyes were almost sunken with grief. He was aware of her pain, and he was watching her closely. On several occasions he thought he would approach his recruit. He had never been asked to expedite training. You can't rush perfection; you can't cut corners. Success depended on those who believe in the attention to detail. He was attentive to Megan, although she hadn't noticed. He was attentive to her language, and she was speaking loudly without saying a word. He heard her loud and clear several times, but he was cautiously optimistic. He had been correct in his assumption, and she was finally finding her way. He could see it, and it was time.

Chad liked to be called "C J." That's how he signed all his electronic messages. He glanced at his phone and didn't see any alerts. He didn't expect there to be. He hadn't received any entry alarm alerts since the security system was installed at his residence. It was a top-notch, wireless, security monitoring system. Recessed infrared cameras were strategically located around his property. There were dummy cameras as well to ward off casual onlookers. State-of-the-art, color-coded, landscape lighting would change when property zone areas were breached during evening hours. There were three different fail-safe entry access codes to include retina, fingerprint, voice activation, and pre-coded numbers that changed by the integrated designed program. An override code was retained by memory only. It was not a system on the market for the rich and famous, although they would be the precise individuals who could afford it. This state-of-the-art platform was governmental covert. Chad was not just any neighbor. The fact of the matter was, he didn't have any close neighbors. The property wasn't his, but belonged to his employers, and it was elaborate. No one had ever entered the interior without prior approval. Very few young and unsuspecting youths had ventured down the lone single-lane, paved road to the property. Warnings of arrest and prosecution were strategically posted on the property. The warnings were serious to anyone who read them. The consequence of trespassing had never been tested. Well, they had once. They were brave, young, foolish teens who never knew the meaning of the word "fear." These boys were determined to impress their girlfriends and proceed beyond the warning signs.

A gate retracted automatically when an authorized vehicle, emitting a programmed frequency, passed over the sensors underneath the pavement surface. The steel gate would retract from left to right at a pace set by the speed of the approaching vehicle. Sensors were staged at 1000 feet and 500 feet, respectively. If the vehicle was traveling at twenty miles per hour or seventy miles per hour, the gate would retract at a pace, relative to the vehicle's approach. The gate would close at the same pace when the vehicle passed. The driver of the vehicle had only to turn on the car radio to a specific station. This frequency would emit the needed transmission allowing safe passage; rather ingenious technology. The public had no idea of the technological, endless possibilities, which were being used to keep them safe. Of course, there was no frequency installed on the car these brave young men were in, therefore it had to pull to a stop. They all climbed out the white 2015 BMW 435i sport coupe. Soon, thereafter, they all learned the definition of the word fear. A full sixty seconds passed after the car pulled to a stop. The Beamer sat on the sensors triggering the security protocol. They were surprised by four bright flashes--two on each side of the road – two facing from the front, two facing from the rear, simulating paparazzi photo ops. Then, came the flash bombs, one on each side of the road. The four teens screamed in fright from the concussion in the night. At about the same time, both exterior mirrors on daddy's prize ride exploded, leaving charred glass on the pavement.

Then, unexpectedly, an authoritative female voice out of nowhere commanded, "This is your last warning; trespassers will be dealt with appropriately."

The warning message was repeated twice, although the teens never heard the second warning. The departing acceleration marks remained on the pavement for weeks.

Off-road access wasn't inviting for the fun and adventurous as well. The terrain kept hikers away, especially with the military-looking warning signs that said prosecution awaited those who proceeded. Small-town rumors traveled fast, and it's believed that following that summer evening, curious onlookers all but ceased to exist.

Chad powered up his computer system. The CPU hummed to life, and the interfaced monitors blinked life in the basement of his modest three-bedroom, three-bath, ranch-style home. The basement was unlike most residences. It had been remodeled to all but hide the door to the basement stairs. There were no basement windows, and the foundation set low on the level, manicured lot. Any unsuspecting onlooker wouldn't realize a large room was beneath the living space.

He typed a short message. It wasn't in code, but to an unsuspecting reader, it might as well have been. It was straight to the point, and a reply was promptly expected at the receiver's earliest opportunity.

"Contact was inadvertently made this afternoon. The prospects are promising."

The email was sent to Dr. Morris, Brian Finch, and cc'd group members of "MoTAF", Missouri Tactical Analysis Force.

Chad Jerguson was a recruiter. His recruiting market was of one, sometimes two, unsuspecting applicants. His job was to recruit smart, unsuspecting, available talent. New hires would be trained to supplement other trained professionals. This employment was voluntary and dangerous. Those recruited were singled out specifically. They were part of a program they had no idea they were being recruited for. They were chosen after being nominated by acquaintances of team associates. The vetting process was exhaustive and lengthy. There weren't any background checks like those done by other employers. Sometimes these recruits took years to develop. They were carefully and unsuspectingly tailored for what was hoped would be successful employment. These applicants were successful in their own rights but weren't aware of their prospective employer. They weren't ever going to seek out this employer because this employer wasn't public and didn't exist until called upon. Megan's career was on track. She didn't realize it, but she was on her way to a potentially well-financed career. All she had to do was accept the offer. The decision was made to put her on the fast track. The worst day of her life catapulted her in the accelerated career path. She had already been vetted but had to be ready for the transition. This program had never been expedited. Megan was about to experience things she never expected. Chad was assigned to recruit her or to be her so-called "handler." Both of her parents had entered her into the program. Her law career would be catapulted at the untimely demise of Emily and Marcus Swift.

Chad added another positive line to his correspondence.

"Aggressive measures will be implemented at the earliest convenience. The applicant is receptive. - C. J."

CHAPTER 5

Terrorism has always been a priority for the law enforcement community. After 9/11, priorities catapulted to the forefront, along with the funding, to finance any efforts to keep Americans safe. That funding was overwhelmingly supported politically as well as privately. Any skepticism voiced by any elected official was sure to cause a firestorm during re-election campaign efforts.

Five years prior to the terror attacks from our foreign enemies, those same efforts to combat evildoers domestically, was met with opposition. Then came April 1995, when Timothy McVeigh became a household name and synonymous with the Alfred P. Murrah Federal Building in Oklahoma City. Much of the time it came down to the almighty dollar. There was a lot of dialogue regarding what must be done, and the necessity of getting it done quickly. Most agreed that security measures needed to be in place, but few agreed on the "who" or "how" to fund it. The more people who became involved, the harder it was to control the purse strings. The bandwagon was full of opinions on either side of the fence, and a few strung out in other places as well. It was as if terrorist attacks occurring on foreign soil, killing or wounding Americans, were acceptable. However, when the threat of innocent children falling victim to terror in our schools and public places, loud voices become clear. The once broad line of financial barriers became paper thin, and grant funding under the umbrella of Homeland Security became commonplace.

Finding those who want to do us harm is not an easy task. It can be like searching for one venomous snake as you are walking through a field of tall grass. There are those snakes in the grass who call themselves "patriots", lurking to strike under the disguise of whatever cause they decide to come up with. One such snake would be the Sovereign Citizen Patriots.

Members of the Sovereign Citizen Patriots called themselves "Patriots". They did not have to do much research for their recruiting base. There was little difficulty finding those who accepted the invitation of ending the tyranny of those they felt were treading on the Constitution. The Patriots drafted legal documents and mailed them to state attorney generals across the U. S. All had ignored the cease and desist document, ordering the relinquishing of powers of their offices to the elected sheriffs in respective counties. Some had publicly voiced oppositions to the so-called Patriots' opposition to governments governing.

No one was more outspoken than Marcus O'Brian, the Libertarian attorney general, from Kentucky. He loudly denounced to every media outlet willing to carry his message of the absurd notions of state office holders vacating their office. General O'Brian boldly broadcast how Patriots were not defenders of any state constitution and should be ashamed to call themselves neighbors of proud veterans, who had served the state of Kentucky and the country with honors. News outlets coddled the attorney general's office. His media communications staff was successful, announcing the open press conference on the steps of the Abraham Lincoln birthplace home, to further his message. It was a well-publicized event, and it was rumored O'Brian was going to announce his candidacy for the highest elected state office-- the governor.

The press conference was slated for 4:00 p.m. on a beautiful Friday. Campaign staff was smart in their scheduling. They knew it would be perfect for his constituents to take off half a day on Friday, getting a jump on their weekend. This, of course, meant getting out of the office most of the day so they could prep for the occasion. There were banners and yard signs lining the road shoulder leading up to the landmark site. It was a short hour-and-a-half drive from the State House to Lincoln Park. The general was traveling by private vehicle to the press conference for the announcement. No state funds were being used to transport the attorney general to any campaign event. That would be political suicide. Regardless, complaints were pouring into the A.G.'s office as well as the governor's office. People just needed to vent about political discourse, and where else but with their elected officials. The announcement had been slated to occur at the federally-funded historical site. He might as well have stood on the steps of a church proclaiming religious freedom.

General O'Brian's white sedan glided down the minimally traveled state road. Today, however, there had been traffic. The two-lane rural highway had been packed with supporters and media to capture the likely top story event for the day, and likely weeks to come. A black Chevrolet Tahoe, with low profile antennas lining the center roof of the SUV, sat waiting at the service entrance for the A.G.'s arrival.

O'Brian was seated in the back, right seat; and his campaign staff seated back left. His communication director sat in the front, right passenger seat. The communications director called the security detail at the venue site and advised them they were twenty-five minutes out. The intern driving was a nephew of the general's special assistant. They were unsuspecting of a vehicle following them. It had been following at a five-car distance and had steadily reduced its speed by two miles per hour per mile for the last ten miles. It had picked them up just minutes from the A.G.'s departure from the State House. The Kentucky state license number "AG-1" was a dead giveaway. The driver of the unknown tail car was one of the attorney general's recent foes--a Sovereign Patriot. The trailing Patriot soldier had notified another solidarity member of their anticipated arrival to the pre-designated location. It had been rehearsed several times, and alternate scenarios were planned in two phases. Phase one was to occur ten miles from Lincoln Park. Phase two was to occur at the park if phase one was unsuccessful.

A text message was sent and received regarding the suspected route of travel, and confirmed via a second text with the approximate speed of travel. A truck, driven by a long-haired blonde, had driven past the event site twice at thirty-minute intervals and hadn't noticed anything different either time. The plain-clothes security officers in the SUV were still sitting at the service entrance to the park, looking down at their cell phones or laptops. It was confirmed via another text from a Patriot soldier planted in the crowd of the would-be entrance for the state attorney general. The pickup was backed up to a farm gate at one of the many fields along the barren highway. Sitting alone in the pick-up truck, the blonde retrieved the heavy payload quadcopter drone from the Samsonite-like cushioned case

A text message alert sounded, and the blonde picked up the phone and read: "15 minutes from ground zero. On cruise 60 MPH. I'm out of the red zone."

The Patriot opened the mapping app on a laptop and viewed the trailing Patriot vehicle as an approaching flashing dot to the drone location. Everything was proceeding according to the plan.

The security detail was expecting a crowd of around 200 invited supporters. The historic site was the backdrop of the largely publicized event. The AG's office requested law enforcement support from the Larue County Sheriff's Department and sent out invites to news outlets statewide. Security knew that meant a huge number of people would be there, and safety of the masses was paramount. There had been briefings during the week, and nothing was left to chance upon the arrival of the attorney general; or so they thought.

The blonde Sovereign Patriot got out of the truck, placing the hard-plastic case in the bed on the open tailgate. The drone was removed from the case and placed in the center of the truck bed. There was no obstructed view of the level, flat road, which was surrounded by soybeans. It was an eerie sound of nothing as far as one could see in either direction; no traffic, no wind. The location was specifically chosen for that reason alone. Another padded case was unlatched, and carefully placed the contents in the bed of the truck next to the drone.

Plastic zip ties attached the payload to the bottom of the drone's landing bracket. There was a planned lift off, but no safe landing site was ever discussed. The payload would detach upon impact from the drone, although the blonde wasn't concerned about the damage. The loss of a drone was simply the cost of doing business.

The pickup driver sat patiently behind the wheel, observing the laptop monitor while holding the drone controller. A different alert sounded loudly on the blonde's laptop, and the drone was promptly powered up and raised slowly out of the bed of the truck to hover fifty feet over the southbound lane. The white sedan could be seen easily on the monitor screen in the pick-up. The monitor read one-fourth mile and closing. The steady hands lowered the drone slowly to 1.3 meters, centering over the lane. Full toggle and the drone sped toward the A.G.'s sedan. The video monitor was showing precise placement, windshield high.

The intern applied the brakes just as he realized something was approaching his windshield. The communication director shouted, causing O'Brian to look up from his review of the prepared speech.

The laptop video screen in the truck faded to black. The blonde glanced up to see the sedan veer off the road into the field, following the drone's impact with the windshield. The blonde turned on the ignition and began to pull out from the grassy field entrance when the explosion occurred. The truck calmly entered the highway, traveling the opposite direction. The trailing vehicle of the AG's sedan turned around, and then began trailing the blonde in the pick-up. The interior of O'Brian's vehicle exploded and overturned several times before coming to rest, right side up. Flames engulfed the SUV in seconds.

The blonde pulled off his wig, and the Patriots followed each other, never to be seen until their next assignment. The wig was thrown behind the truck cab seat. The pickup and chase car returned to the rural safe havens of the "Show-Me State".

CHAPTER 6

Megan had grown up somewhat sheltered. She had learned how to take care of herself but was never tested. Her father taught her how to handle the firearm she received as a gift from her parents. She enjoyed going to the range with both her mom and dad. It was one of the family things they did together. She particularly enjoyed the talks she had, either with both parents or individually. Discipline and focus were her foundation, and she knew very well from where that fortitude came. She had a grasp on being safe because it was something her parents had instilled in her. She willfully admitted to her parents that bad things only happened in places where they were supposed to happen; nothing ever happened where they lived.

Megan removed her jeans and t-shirt from her gym bag and slung them on her bed. She thought of her grocery list. She would make her trip to Sam's or Walmart another day. Her shopping list wasn't long because she shopped modestly. Bulk items carried her through several weeks, which was her goal. It kept her from being in public. She had grown to dislike crowds over the past several months and knew it was something she hadn't had a problem with before. She would just go out another time and get the things she needed.

"Recovery, a work in progress," she uttered out loud.

She kicked her cross-trainer tennis shoes to the corner of the room, grabbed two clothes hangers from her closet, and hung up her jeans and t-shirt. Leaving all other items in her bag, she made her way to the shower. She unlocked the screen on her cell phone and opened the Pandora app and navigated to a 'wake up' genre. The music was like the sound track from the historic movie "Rocky," starring Sylvester Stallone. She wasn't going for a run; she was taking a shower. She used to listen to music while bathing. Recently however, she just climbed in and out from under the pulsating streams without any forethought. It was a routine she hadn't thought anything about until now. She opened the cabinet and fumbled under the sink, looking for her wireless speaker. Finding it, she hit the power switch and smiled when the activation tone sounded. Her smile was twofold. She was surprised to hear the speaker power up and she realized that she was, in fact, smiling. The speaker hadn't been used for so long, she figured the battery had to be charged. It had also been a while since she cracked a smile just for the sake of smiling. Her emotional battery not only needed charging, but replaced with a DieHard. She cranked up the volume and pressed the suction cup on the bottom of the speaker to the shower wall. She grabbed her towel and tossed it in the hamper. She had been using the same one for over a week and wondered why she hadn't replaced it. It made her think of the towel in her locker at the Y. It was way past due for replacing. She wondered what others could be thinking as they walked by locker thirty-five, all the while turning up their noses. It was her favorite number assigned to her when playing basketball in high school.

She grabbed a fresh towel from the linen closet. After stripping down, she rolled her knee length gym shorts into a ball and tossed them to the hamper. She missed her mark.

"I'll bank it next time," she said out loud, as she tiptoed across the floor picking up her clothes.

Throwing her clothes into the hamper was not part of any routine, and she knew it. Any part of picking up after herself was a chore; something she hated, and therefore just didn't care to do. Climbing under the lukewarm, pulsating stream, she began to sing and sing out loud. It was the first time in months she had even thought about the possibility of running out of hot water. It seemed like an eternity since she'd taken a long soul-searching shower like the one she was now taking.

Wrapping herself in the fleece, beach-like towel, she nearly dried her hair without using the blow dryer. Standing in front of the body length mirror, staring at herself, she knew it was time. Should she trim it and have the split ends nipped, or maybe just cut it? She had seen some cute, short styles and had wondered what they would look like on her.

She continued to stare. "What are you doing to yourself?" she said in a soft whisper and smiled. Those were words her mother would say to her when she was at her low moments. Her mom always seemed to pull her out of any dark abyss she found herself in. She missed her terribly.

She was beginning to think she should have showered at the gym and eaten out because her meal choice was limited. The evening passed quickly after her quick sensible supper. She felt perhaps an Aleve would be a smart move to minimize any morning-after stiffness that was sure to follow the day's workout. She may have overdone it, but it felt so right. Deciding not to be a wimp, she skipped the pain meds. She struggled out of her skinny-fit ankle cropped jeans before folding them on the recliner next to her bed. She threw on her dad's oversized MIZZOU t-shirt she used for pajamas. She loved that shirt. She loved how it made her feel because her dad would purposely wear it every time she came home from college. Megan knew she wasn't going out after grabbing supper that evening and didn't normally get dressed like she was expecting company. Her norm for many months resembled that of a hermit. Today was different. She opened her fridge and, by instinct, pulled from the shelf door a vanilla Ensure protein drink. The coolness felt inviting to the touch in anticipation of her favorite flavor.

She threw herself on the bed, and then stretched to grab her laptop from the end table. Grabbing the TV remote, she settled comfortably in pursuit of the sights and sounds that filled the echoes of her quiet, three-bedroom house. The silence became a familiarity before crying herself to sleep. The tears eventually stopped even when she wanted them to flow. After today, she knew for the first time she was going to be alright. It was time to catch up on much needed correspondence. It was not something she was looking forward to, but for some reason, she felt she was up to it. Then it happened. The television caught her attention, although she was not listening or even looking at it, --a preliminary report from the trusted KY3 news.

"We turn to one of our sister stations, KYZX in Frankfort, Kentucky for some breaking, investigative news." The picture switched to an apparent recording of the scene of a traffic crash.

"A horrific traffic crash occurring on a rural highway has taken the life of the Kentucky Attorney General. General O'Brian was en route to the National Historic Birthplace of Abraham Lincoln. The Libertarian

Attorney General reportedly was expected to launch his candidacy for Governor. The car General O'Brian was riding in was driven by an intern working for his office."

The television news reporter was standing across a highway, showing a badly charred vehicle resting in a field. "Stay tuned for updates of more breaking news."

The video then scanned the scene with the reporter standing near flashing, emergency lights and what appeared to be firemen in the backdrop.

Megan closed her laptop, turned off the TV, and then turned off the softly lit table lamp next to her. She took a deep breath and closed her eyes, trying to find solace in something that would allow her to sleep through the night. She pondered the loss of her parents. She felt stiffness in her shoulders and thought she needed the Aleve, but willed herself to stay in bed.

"I need to adjust my upper body workout," remembering why the tightness was there.

He was cute and focused on his workout, and not on any other women in the gym. "Maybe I could use a workout buddy," she thought. The corners of her mouth turned up in a smile, and then turned to a frown as she recalled the news scene, which must have resembled the one that had changed her life forever. She closed her eyes and drifted off to sleep.

CHAPTER 7

Chad always set the timer on his coffee pot. It made sense for him to have it ready and waiting when he woke. He put together his familiar breakfast fruit plate. He was low on kiwi and made a mental note to himself. He walked past the study to the clandestine basement. His work study on the main floor of the modest ranch style home had a desk, computer, and printer but was rarely used. He became accustomed to the confines of "the cave". His personal computer was linked to his work study in the basement, if he desired not to venture downstairs.

The hallway coat and broom closet were an add-on feature to the home. He never hung any coats there, but it was perfect for the brooms and vacuum cleaner. It was slightly larger in width to allow for the back wall to recess into the hallway framework. This made it easy for Chad to carry his breakfast tray with coffee and juice. He turned on the big screen TV, where he had his favorites programmed into the remote. He kept abreast on all the top newsworthy issues. His main interests were all the national networks. He programmed them by order of interest starting with Fox News, MSNBC, and CNN. Recently, however, he had tired of them all and was seriously considering changing the order of importance. Politics was boring him badly. Campaigning, starting eighteen months out from a presidential election year, was more than he could stomach. It was amazing to him how anyone could remain interested that long. He was convinced none of it made any difference until late in the cycle when major political parties had their convention nominations. He was bracing himself for more of the same when out of habit, he muted the volume.

He took his men's multivitamins to start off his morning routine.

He was preparing for the morning political rhetoric; however, it didn't happen during this news cycle. He had already turned his back to the TV programming, concentrating on his computer monitor and email. He was hoping there would be a response to email he sent the previous day. His responses were there.

There were two emails, and he opened the first one from Brian Finch, which was sent at 9:06 p.m. He wondered if any of these people ever slept. Chad was another one who kept late hours. He routinely combed through his email and responded at all hours of the night, although he hadn't the previous evening. He checked his anti-virus software and the status reports of the scans that ran through the evening hours. No threats out of the ordinary. He began reading the email from Brian Finch, the investment banker.

"We must continue to follow the plan, and you'll be fine," his email started. "We are being forced to move perhaps faster than we all would prefer, especially now. It is not our choice the pace has quickened. She will inquire to what you do for a living, and you'll cunningly encourage her to wonder about more. Your vagueness could cause her to follow her instincts, promptly kicking you to the curb."

Brian was always the jokester, and his wittiness served him well. Chad didn't understand his mention about moving up the timeline more than it already was.

"Chad, prepare the boardroom for an emergency meeting for MoTAF. We've got to get in front of the Kentucky attorney general's death," Chad noticed the email was copied to Dr. Morris and MoTAF. "We will discuss Ms. Swift's progress at the board meeting. Plan on bringing something to eat for lunch."

"Crap, an emergency board meeting. What the heck is he talking about, and what happened in Kentucky?" Chad thought out loud and then opened the email from Dr. Morris.

"I'm pleased to learn of the progress Megan has made. Chad, we all entrust her to your professional insight."

Chad received his undergraduate psychological behavioral courses online. He targeted that academia for his profession; until he, too, was recruited several years prior.

"Continue to keep us informed of her well-being. I have a particular interest in her mental state. Your psychology and social counseling background will serve us well in this endeavor. See you soon." Chad turned around and grabbed the remote.

Every national news channel had its own network contributors analyzing the ramifications of the attorney general's death. Chad found himself glued to the television, switching to every channel on his favorite's list getting a different version of the traffic accident. Chad was wanting to mute the TV again, as it was turning into sideshow after sideshow. It was amazing how a tragic traffic accident turned to legislation being drafted to disallow interns to work with candidates seeking elected offices. It was as if the college student wasn't capable of driving elected officials because of the enormous responsibility.

Chad again focused on the emails he received and began thinking about what was needed to prepare for the meeting. Although there was constant communication with people of MoTAF, it hadn't been since the attack of 9/11 that a board meeting had been called. One-on-one meetings were not normally conducted or deemed necessary. It was Chad's responsibility to obtain as much inside information as he could about the incident, formulate a synopsis, and determine what effect, if any, it would have on the security front in Missouri. Chad was an attention-to-detail type of guy.

MoTAF employees were scattered all over the state. Employees were unaware of how many others were working with the agency. They were confident; however, missions of homeland security were being fulfilled. Chad walked to the wall safe hidden behind a 15" X 20" framed picture of Academic Hall, the historic columns of the first building on the campus of the University of Missouri. He spun the dial on the combination lock and retrieved a binder. The binder contained the name and contact information of other employees. Chad was MoTAFs' analyst, and it was time for him to begin analyzing. He flipped through the tabs of states listed in alphabetical order stopping at Kentucky. Picking up his Android, he unlocked the screen and called his analyst counterpart. They had spoken before, but not frequently as there was no reason to. He began his inquiry and learned why a meeting had been called. The Kentucky contact informed him that the incident taking the life of the Kentucky attorney general was no accident. The news wires had speculated on the cause of the traffic crash and exploited the comments from investigators at the scene, who were speaking on the condition of anonymity. The cause was not inattention by the youthful driver.

Chad learned his contact received a preliminary cause of death of an occupant in the SUV. The driver had been riddled with shrapnel, as if he had been standing in front of a Claymore mine when it went off. Because of the intense heat from the fire, little could be determined as to the cause of the crash. There was no forensic discovery. No one thought there was malice involved in an unfortunate accident. If not for witnesses when the attorney general departed the State House, the identity of occupants would have taken several days, if not weeks. The families wanted to mourn and put the tragic, and soon-to-be Kentucky historic event behind them. The SUV was crushed and found its way to a recycling company. There would be no souvenir collectors making profit from this tragedy. Historians would perhaps write some articles, craft some lapel pins, or buttons with slogans of a man never to be forgotten. Perhaps there would be approval and final passage of a bill to erect a bust resembling the attorney general in the halls of the State House. The other passengers would be lucky to get an asterisk behind their name as a footnote in any historical pamphlet, book or magazine.

Analysts from the Department of Homeland Security were forwarding information to the underground network as fast as they could obtain it. Each state had its own office of Homeland Security. Most were crafted from grants out of the September 11 framework. Missouri was the first state to draft such an agency. What people didn't realize was the network went underground from the state to rid itself of red tape. Like most bureaucratic strongholds, the upper echelon is generally able to forecast and see the bigger picture and, therefore, apply resources where they are most beneficial. Using a historical perspective, mistakes are less likely to reoccur. History was the best teacher. However, like so many things, the perspective gets lost, ideals become over-reaching, and the mission changes in the grand scheme. Port bill funding finds its way to specific congressional districts or worse, mortgages get paid off, and vacation homes in exotic places get built.

MoTAF had no issues for becoming too large or the mission getting lost in the shuffle. Data would be sifted through and analyzed multiple times to come up with enough evidence to do what was needed. At present, all data seemed to point in one direction, and it appeared little was being done to hide the perpetrators' intentions. To the outside world, their mayhem would be hidden.

Chad, using a spreadsheet, began combining the data finding similarities that sent chills up his spine. The assault on the Kentucky general was well planned and carried out. He hadn't seen anything like it, and what concerned him was it appeared the attack wasn't the first attempt. The first was foiled by the unsuspected change in the general's schedule. It was impressive how well organized the network of hate had become. It was concerning that the network had a strong foothold in the "Show-Me State". You truly didn't know whom you could trust.

CHAPTER 8

Megan woke surprisingly rested. It had become normal not to get a full night's sleep. She made her way to the bathroom, splashing cool water on her face. It would be a good morning run. The only decision would be if it would be an extended run or kept at a normal pace and distance. She wanted plenty of energy for her afternoon workout. Looking forward to something was out of the ordinary. It was the mid-sixties, unseasonably cool, but perfect for her run. She got dressed, tightly wrapped her hair in a ponytail, then untied it, and let it hang. Shaking her head, like a wet dog coming out of a pond, her hair draped to both sides past her jaw line, just past her shoulders. It was too long, and it was time to decide which style fit her best. It had to be manageable and cute. She tied it back again and made her way to the middle of her living room floor to stretch. Her mind was racing to all the things she thought she could possibly get accomplished during the day. It was turning out to be a normal day of nothings, but she was okay with that.

Springing to her feet, bouncing back to the bedroom, she grabbed her hip-hugging, concealment jogging carrier. She slid her GLOCK in the elastic Velcro pocket, opened the Pandora app on her phone, and then slid it in the elastic pocket on the belt. She grabbed her keys and ID and firmly pressed her molded earbuds into each ear.

She wasn't going to run her normal three miles. She liked her tea and planned on rewarding herself with a quick stop at the Price Cutter Starbucks. Breathing deep to catch her breath, she stretched outside the entryway, trying to do a quick cool down before entering the grocery store. A mental list of things to be done was formulating in her mind as she read the advertisements lining the store windows. Her "to do" list for the day was increasing, particularly the grocery shopping.

"Hi, Ms. Swift!" Brian sounded cheerful as he approached the automatic door entryway. He noticed her standing near the parking lot concrete support base for the light pole.

"Hello," was her simple response with a quizzical look.

The face was familiar, but it wasn't an easy recollection. Perhaps it was the sunglasses or the nice dark blue pinstripe suit. His tie was bright red with a backdrop of a light blue button-down, colored shirt. He definitely was a businessman who was undoubtedly on his way to work. He could tell by the look on her face that she had no clue who he was.

"You don't remember me, do you?" he said with a smile. He extended his hand for a quick shake and reintroduction. He took off his UV Oakley sunglasses, and smiled. "How's this? I'll take off my disguise."

"Oh my gosh, I'm sorry. I should have recognized you." She still was at a loss, and was trying to come up with a way to ask his name.

He still noticed the puzzled look on her face and gave her an out by introducing himself again.

"Brian Finch. It's not like we see each other all that often." He could see the relaxed posture as she bowed her head as if embarrassing herself. "I thought perhaps you were going to call me to go over the insurance information I gave you. It can be overwhelming."

"I do need to do that," she smartly recovered and with a grin. "I was thinking about making some changes, like perhaps buying myself a car."

"That would probably be a good idea. I don't think you can run everywhere you want to go," gesturing to her attire.

"Exactly!" she smiled. Another customer exiting caused the automatic door to slide open.

"After you," Brian stepped aside allowing her to go before him. They both walked to the Starbucks counter.

"Here for your morning mojo?" she said, while unzipping a pouch in her jogging belt.

"Like minds I suppose," Brian quipped.

"No, I just came for my tea fix. I decided to take a short break before I finish my run."

Brian had thought about offering to buy but decided it would be a little forward under the circumstances. She had no idea of what was potentially available to her. Her law career could be on track if she wanted, as well as a career she was unaware of. A decision would soon be made as to how quickly things would proceed with her. He was uncomfortable with her not knowing about him being part of something she would soon be invited to participate. He was, however, excited about what was in store for her. Things were being fast tracked, especially after the Kentucky crash.

A familiar sound could be heard from a distance. An ambulance or fire truck was screaming in their direction. They could hear the sirens getting closer from inside the store. Both tried to ignore the obvious, but the lull in the conversation caused them both to glance at the traffic light intersection. An ambulance and police cruiser slowly navigated through the intersection on an emergency run. They both stood silently for a moment not knowing what to say or how to exit their awkwardness. Both understood the likelihood of someone's misfortune occurring at that very moment. Brian handed her his business card.

"Call me soon. I'd be more than happy to answer any questions you have, maybe even give you some ideas on what car you should trade for those tennis shoes."

"Thank you. I will. I promise."

She sipped on her iced tea while he walked away. She waved as he turned to look at her while getting in his car. She quickly finished her iced tea and tossed her cup in the trash. She noticed he lingered in his car for an awkward timeframe looking down undoubtedly at his phone. He looked at her once again, smiling as he pulled from the lot. She felt overly rested due to her extended break, one that she hadn't planned on. She wondered if the return run home might be more difficult than she anticipated.

CHAPTER 9

Sovereign Citizen Patriots had taken it upon themselves to commit the most heinous of crimes and make it look otherwise. Preventing crimes against government and the attempted dismantling of democracy were never more paramount. The MoTAF meeting was arranged, and all responded in the affirmative to the noon gathering. It was going to be a short turn-around after being notified of the meeting and the actual date and time to be there.

They all rehearsed this scenario in their minds many times over. The artifice would be of a family emergency occurring, which they had to be present for. The return would be explained away by a crafty false alarm. Each MoTAF member was employed in a multitude of different professions. An abrupt leave of absence had to be created for circumstances just as what was occurring. The internal data-gathering fiber of MoTAF had lit up. All resources were combing all trusted avenues of discovering the who, the how, and the why. It resembled using a multitude of confidential informants for the conclusion of a successful drug investigation. The network was working flawlessly, and the world of intelligence-gathering was at its best. Because ground zero was Kentucky, the analyst had contacted his D.C. counterparts. The network was amazingly effective. Moonlighters from law clerks within the United States Supreme Court, analysts from Homeland Security, FBI, and the CIA were part of a meticulous woven spider web. No egos ever surfaced, although one would be naïve to think they did not exist.

Brian worked his magic, and the meeting place was ready. It took hours, but packets containing up-to-date information not yet released to media were ready for viewing. The information was forwarded to him from his counterpart in Kentucky. Brian had put together the information, which resembled terrorism chatter from communicating networks. This chatter wasn't the threatening of mayhem to all infidels from far away Afghanistan, but it was just as serious. It was just as believable as if it was coming from a radicalized Islamic State. The D.C. network had picked up confirmation from overzealous unknowns. There wasn't any doubt that the Kentucky attorney general had made some bold statements upsetting anti-governmental proponents.

The chatter coming from social media information openly discussed how "the cats' claws were removed"… "cats will no longer climb onto any more nets or hang from any rims."

These people were professionals for successfully pulling off the unthinkable. They were perhaps also juvenile in their triumph march. A reference to Kentucky Wildcats basketball could be a break in determining who was behind the murders.

The analysts from Homeland Security picked up the reference by searching all the social media networks. The usernames were different, but some were obviously the same person. Computer software modules searched for similarities in language usage, pronunciations, grade-level of usage, and sentence structure. There were many similarities in the rants coming through social media. It wasn't going to be easy finding this needle in an oversized haystack.

One example of the most boisterous rhetoric came from an IP address tracked to a student attending Southeast Missouri University (SEMO). A courtesy visit was made to this young man from the local FBI office. Like many young men, Brody Wesson, had the world's view in his grasp. Especially better than those above the age of thirty. He had a thing or two he was willing to enlighten the agents on. He was being asked to willingly discuss his knowledge, if any, of the traffic crash taking the life of the Kentucky Attorney General. The young student was informed about how his Twitter comments got the attention of some very interested government officials. The agents were soon enlightened about the First and Second amendments.

Brody explained, "As a law student and U.S. citizen, I can say what I want, when I want, and you federal guys can't control the Internet."

The agents were apologetic and in agreement to his First Amendment rights. Both agents came away confident the first-year law student from Kentucky had no knowledge of anything other than what he saw on television or recently read. The agents left the campus dorm smugly knowing full well, this student would learn firsthand of the long reaching resources the FBI have at their disposal.

Within the week, an anonymous tip to the campus police had a drug canine sniffing around the boisterous SEMO student's white, 1993 Ford Bronco. It was eerily similar to the one O.J. Simpson was notoriously riding in when captured on video played over and over during slow-motion police pursuit on the LA freeway. That pursuit is forever etched in our minds, as the scene that was witnessed by college classmates of a young freshman led out of class by campus police to his car.

The campus police explained to Brody, how the university administration had a zero tolerance of illicit drugs on campus. The dean of academic affairs just happened to be present, awaiting the student's escorted arrival from class. The campus police were requesting permission to search, and campus administration was present to witness the search. Brody was informed about the tip received about his trafficking drugs and contraband from the vehicle they were all standing around. He confirmed the Bronco was his but assured everyone that he did not loan his car to anyone, and there were no drugs in it. The canine officer explained to the student that his dog hit on his vehicle. The Dutch shepherd lay near a rear tire and in the shade of the Bronco, with its leash firmly in hand of the campus canine officer. It was readily apparent, even to the first-year law student, what was occurring. The dean was patiently waiting for the student's waiver to search. The young man protested he wasn't signing anything, but they could search all they wanted because he had nothing to hide. A small crowd of students lingered near, as the vehicle was unlocked.

Brody boldly stated, "Does this have anything to do with my visit from the FBI?"

The dean, and officers present, gave each other a quizzical look. Brody turned away from the stares avoiding the obvious, they had no idea about his surprise visit.

Dr. Andrews, Dean of Academic Affairs, stood at Brody's shoulder. "We will discuss this matter later in my office."

After several minutes, no drugs were found, but the dog hinted on several areas of the vehicles interior. The snickering from onlookers was humiliating in and of itself.

"Brody," Dr. Andrews spoke in an authoritative tone, "be in my office first thing in the morning."

~ ~ ~

The following morning, Brody nervously sat, explaining how he was positive drugs were never in his vehicle. Dr. Andrews lowered his chin, glancing down at the folder containing several papers.

"We have a zero-tolerance illicit drug policy the administration strongly upholds." Dr. Andrews continued, "I strongly suggested you keep better friends to joy ride around with, or secure your vehicle when you leave it."

Brody was shocked to learn his work-study on campus had been revoked, and his scholarship had been suspended indefinitely. Brody Wesson would soon be transferring to another school or dropping out altogether. He was smart enough to know it was all because of the comments made on his Twitter account and speaking his mind to the FBI.

CHAPTER 10

The chartered flight came from D.C. It made a stop in Frankfort, Kentucky, and Columbia, Missouri before landing at Branson/ Springfield, Missouri General Aviation. Brian met them at the terminal, and they took the twenty-five-minute drive to Chad's residence. There wasn't much of an agenda for the noon board meeting, nor a mission statement mounted on any wall to be read by those entering. There was just an understanding by a board of commission that worked out of a rural southwest Missouri residence. A mission statement was listed on the cover page of briefings and was also electronically transmitted to members who were to be in attendance. It was a reminder of the seriousness of the mission and how it must be successful at all cost and always. When a board meeting was called, which was extremely rare, briefings were in print for those attending. The mission statement was part of the documents at the meeting. It read:

"The men and women of MoTAF are dedicated to preserve freedom and democracy within the boundaries of the United States. This mission will not be taken lightly by those who have sworn to uphold it. Those who propose to alter the will of the people shall be dealt with extreme prejudice. There will be no afterthought of the welfare of the perpetrator/s. The consequences of their own actions will be the elimination of their existence. The resolve of our state relies in the resiliency of those protecting it."

The analyst from Kentucky opened with greetings and got right to the issue at hand. It was determined the likely cause of the traffic accident was the loss of control of the vehicle. Injuries were likely sustained prior to it veering off the road. There were what appeared to be plastics, as well as metal pellets resembling ball bearings, in the remains of all the crash victims. The intense heat from the fire resulted in loss of any potential evidence. The assistant fire marshal on duty concurred with firemen at the scene, who reported the likely overturning of the vehicle and rupturing of the fuel line caused the vehicle fire. Coupled with the fact there was no reason to believe foul play was involved, the family released the vehicle for scrap. There were no witnesses to the accident other than the lone volunteer fireman traveling on the desolate highway. He noticed the smoke as he was approaching and thought it was a farm tractor on fire. The car was nearly melted indescribably. The coroner was contacted by an analyst, who smartly convinced him of her credentials and the seriousness of matters involving Homeland Security. The call to the coroner was made from an untraceable phone number to inquire more about the crash. He was convinced to hold off on officially recording the findings on the cause of the crash occurring in his county. Due to an issue involving national security, he would be contacted regarding his findings. The analyst assured the coroner he would be rewarded for his assistance and professionalism and would be contacted soon. That would be the last they spoke on the matter. The coroner would be waiting indefinitely for a call that would never come.

The analyst followed the meeting agenda, informing his counterparts the networks threatening public officials were being tracked. The suspected threat was to have taken place on a date, which was that of the attorney general's death. Nothing that sinister could be a coincidence. The networks were doing everything possible to narrow down the origin of the threat while attempting to identify specifics of any potential harm to any elected officials. Only so much could be done, if anything at all, with preventing anything in the future.

There was only speculation of how everything transpired. Several theories were contemplated on how the crash occurred, one theory being of a remote device possibly placed on the vehicle and detonated by cell phone frequency. Another idea was of a decoy motorist broken down and the general's car came upon it. Discussion immediately interjected describing the overturning of the car at highway speeds. Another was of a propelled rocket fired at the car and detonating upon impact. The Kentucky analyst explained that they may never know how it occurred or even who the assailant/s were.

The analyst continued by explaining the contact at SEMO was, in fact, a good lead into solving the who and how question. Proving it and exposing their clandestine efforts of defending Missouri's citizenry was always a balancing act. The D.C. contacts procured FBI identification, and local agents were accommodating to those acting under the umbrella of national security to interview the student. The student's Instagram account was deleted, but he remained active on other social media and remained vocal, although somewhat reserved. The decision to interrupt his education was to hopefully gain more insight into activities of the Sovereign Citizen Patriots. The student would unknowingly assist with protecting innocent lives. Encrypted tracking software was uploaded to his IP address. There wasn't any firewall protection on the open market that would recognize, stop, or warn unsuspecting Internet users of the intrusion. Although he wasn't aware, the government whom he vehemently despised, owned him.

The networks were boasting about the victims of the crash deserving of their fate. Underground networks also served as a Patriot recruitment tool. They were growing in numbers, although they appeared to remain small. The board members learned how Patriots would sign into an underground site built solely for communication. The members were smart enough not to comment about any wrongdoing but were careless in communicating about the event before it became public. D.C. analysts were recruited themselves. It was decided early on to become part of a sting operation into the Sovereign Citizen Patriots' network. This was one of many memberships D.C. analysts were part of. The Patriots were among the first to have an underground system for communication as well as for felonious operations. It was quickly gaining momentum, unlike many other networks, second only to the Islamic State in Syria, ISIS. The reason was obvious, following their bragging rights but just falling short of claiming responsibility for the deaths of the attorney general and the three other passengers.

"The Patriots are becoming extremely active," stated the Kentucky analyst. "We're going to need eyes on these guys when they move again."

"Once we get some idea of their intentions," Chad began. "I have some ideas of how we can proceed. Until then, anyone is a sitting duck."

The Kentucky analyst continued mentioning the bullet points in the briefing notes. He referenced how Patriots were talking about moving north to send more messages to nonbelievers.

"We have eyes and ears inside the networks," continued the Kentucky analyst. "We can't motivate or suggest any illicit activity, but we can solidify their intentions and perhaps infiltrate."

"Now we're talking," Chad said enthusiastically. "We've got to move on these guys, or we can just as well be the reason they are successful in their next terror attack."

"I think I know where you're going with this, Chad," Dr. Morris began. "I'm not so sure a recruit is something we should risk, knowing how dangerous these guys are."

"We're all aware how dangerous keeping our state safe can be," Brian continued. "Now is not the time to leave anything to chance. We've got to act and act now."

"Can you be sure our recruit is ready? We can't risk failure."

"We can't risk not being successful. We're essentially saying the same thing. I recommend we move forward with our recruit," Brian interjected. "We're going to need some help with this, and it could get dicey."

"Agreed," said Dr. Morris. "We don't even know how many we're dealing with, how they got to them without being seen, and how they got away."

"Correct," the Kentucky analyst said. "No witnesses, no anything."

"I'll get with our recruit at the earliest opportunity, perhaps today," said Chad. "I'm headed to the gym this afternoon."

"Understood," continued Dr. Morris. "If our recruit shows any sign of reluctance we have to reconsider. We can't afford a new member to become a victim of mistakes made at this juncture."

"Ted, I know how sensitive you are of this prospect," Brian began. "You were in her presence more than any of us. Under the circumstances, we all are sensitive to her well-being. Her participation could be a lasting legacy."

The SEMO blogger had taken down his website, but his hatred for the government had intensified. He spread more hatred and vowed to help those who shined light on the corrupt. The intelligence analysts were gathering threats and assessing the validity regionally, and across the U.S. The Midwest was a hotbed following the so-called accident. There had been the same menial threats on the networks, but nothing warranted more attention than normal until after the accident. D.C. analysts were lamenting how they may have missed something that could have saved lives on that lone, rural highway.

The Kentucky contact was notified of elevated threats during the meeting. Some were specifically directed to Missouri but were general in nature. The intelligence community was gathering information at a feverish pace, which got the attention of Capitol Hill. Alert memos and notifications were sent out to heads of states. After the letters were received from the Sovereign Citizen Patriots and the Kentucky incident, security protocols were recommended to be put into action.

"I got a text from D.C.," the Kentucky analyst looked at Chad. "There is a media loop being played from your governor's office. Turn on the TV; it's something we need to discuss."

Chad grabbed the remote and was switching channels trying to find what the governor had said. The noon hour had passed, and there were no interruptions of regular programming. Chad switched to streaming network channels through satellite feeds. He found what he was looking for, the NBC Political Pulse. It wasn't live programming, but resembled YouTube, where you could search a video to watch the most recent news event in the country.

The Missouri political video was the most recent and one of the top choices to view without having to do a search.

"There it is," said the Kentucky analyst. "That's our state flag with the black ribbons hanging on the pole."

They all watched the video and listened to commentators giving their opinion of the announcement. Chad switched to two more video feeds of the same press conference but with different camera views and different takes on what it meant, if anything, for Missourians.

Ted said, "Well, that will open the flood gates for hate mongers."

"I agree," Brian quipped. "He just drew a line in the sand. That's a standing invitation for anybody to try to remove him from office."

"His security detail will not like that idea," Chad mentioned, as he shook his head in disappointment. "Don't they know what they're doing when they spout off like that?"

"Not a chance. Our A.G. was the most boisterous of them all, and he didn't have a protective shield," the Kentucky analyst added. "He made a lot of people mad and wasn't concerned about toning it down if the polls were in his favor."

"At least he's honoring your A.G.," said Ted. "That's nice of him to sit in front of your state flag."

"Yes, it was, but keep in mind, he was wanting to be Kentucky's next governor. He was rising in the polls by talking conservative and pushing right-wing extremist buttons."

"Exactly," said Ted. "He acknowledged in a press conference, although he didn't come right out and say it, that he, too, received the letter from the Sovereign Citizen Patriots."

"That he did," continued Brian. "With him having a press conference to pay respects to a state office holder is one thing. In the political arena, he just told all who would listen, he agreed with what all the Kentucky A.G. stood for."

"That's problematic," said Chad. "If the press asked, he must have done a good job of sidestepping the question, or we would be watching a sound bite on that as well."

The Kentucky analyst started receiving encrypted alert messaging. Then at the same time, the remaining people in the room got the same encrypted alerts.

"The radical bloggers are lighting up their websites all over," stated the Kentucky analyst. "D.C. is all over it, but it appears you guys are now in the crosshairs of the Sovereign Citizen Patriots."

Before the meeting would be adjourned, a review of emergency protocol was discussed. They all reviewed rules of engagement, and how they were to be implemented if needed. MoTAF created a red, white, and blue code system. The red, white, and blue codes hadn't been used since the 9/11 attacks. Code Red meant high alert. Code White meant remain vigilant, and Code Blue meant stand down. They remained on Code Blue for years, downgraded from red to white, following the Twin Tower attacks. They had been in the blue stand-down mode since the capture of Saddam Hussein. No one thought they would go from blue to red so quickly. Missouri was now Code Red, along with Kentucky. Other states had been elevated to Code White.

They were also sending allegiance notifications through the encrypted alert system, offering any assistance in any fight that would come Missouri's way.

There were communities all over the United States acting on their own behalf, preserving the sanctity of democracy. These organizations were just as concerned with what was going on in their own backyard and were vigilant to keeping those lawns smartly manicured. Those organizations were not financed or trained for front line confrontations. They were sound in keeping their elected officials accountable to their promises. There were forces, however, just as adamant on dismantling what was morally right with the country. It was those forces that needed to be eradicated.

Many years prior, there were discussions on whether an abbreviated vetting of a recruit could be accomplished. It looked as if now would be the practical time to shore up help by whatever means necessary. It normally took years; this was being done in an abbreviated version. The time-table had been moved up once more. There were discussions whether MoTAF could safely recover being compromised. Everyone came to a consensus that risks had to be taken, and nothing was more pressing than what they were now experiencing. No member of MoTAF was careless in their keeping operations clandestine. MoTAF never had a female on the front lines of defense on their team. They were comprised, however, of men and women of all ages and backgrounds.

Chad knew Megan could be a promising addition. He didn't exactly like being deceptive to get close to her, but he was following the plan. It had never failed MoTAF before, and he was sure it wouldn't this time either. A system had been in place for years. Everyone knew the purpose and even knew of its origin and the catalyst that brought the mission to fruition. Most didn't care what brought them to help fill the mission, they just wanted to be part of something meaningful – something that made a difference.

There are those who defend our country within Homeland Security, as well as those under the umbrella of the Pentagon. The list can be long and exhausting of those sworn to defend and protect others. There are no known facets more clandestine than that of MoTAF. The tragedy, which brought the Brady Bill to the floor of the U.S. Congress, is forever ingrained in the history books around the world. It was because of the slow response of the attempted assassination of President Ronald Regan that brought like minds together. It was the verdict under the disguise of reasonable insanity, which caused a strong, meaningful force to respond to action.

A silent group of like-minded people were compelled to do something positive and covertly to ensure peace within our communities. Then came September 11, 2001. The same like-minds found renewed life to be comforters for those who were unsure of their safety. The mission remained the same, but the resolve became more focused and a strong force within their communities and across the United States. MoTAF was that force.

The meeting ended with very little chatting. Things were all business, and everyone understood they would meet again soon. They even discussed possibly having quarterly meetings to discuss, in-person, the state of affairs and what intelligence-gathering other states had acquired that could further their mission.

Chad was invited to accompany the attendees back to the airport. A courtesy call was made to the pilot with an ETA of their return to the airport. They learned his flight plan had already been logged, and he was just awaiting their arrival. They discussed the recruit and some of the potential benefits of her joining MoTAF. They all learned how similar operations were extremely successful. That was the primary reason a recruit was being considered and had been vetted. The recruit had not been approached, and they were all on board regarding the extraordinary circumstances they found themselves in. All admitted they were excited to be involved in potential hands-on, counter-terrorism efforts.

Chad and Brian watched the sleek Learjet taxi onto the runway. They both were sure this would not be the last they would see the D.C. tail number, 779MLT, land or take off from Springfield/Branson International.

Chad and Brian talked further during the drive from the airport about the uncertainty of what could possibly occur, if anything. They knew being prepared was the best defense they had in halting any attempt at terrorism within the state. They discussed the plan in its infancy stages and how they were entering uncharted waters as far as they were concerned.

"There are plenty of modules out there to follow," Brian said. "We're not exactly inventing the wheel here."

"I agree. I just haven't done anything like this, and we all knew she was going to be schooled into the fold through her parents," uttered Chad.

"Things obviously changed," Brian replied.

"You can say that again. She appears to be moving on with her life. We will soon know for sure. I'm heading to the gym today."

Megan had no idea her life was about to take a dramatic turn. She once had a promising law career. A career she had prepared long and hard for. A career, she knew, for which her parents had sacrificed. She was unaware of the type of career path that had been put in place on her behalf or where it would lead. Her law career remained tangible; she just hadn't realized it yet. It was unknowingly put on a different path. She would have to choose: would that path be one she would want for herself, or would her fragile foothold crumble beneath her?

CHAPTER 11

Ruben Zuloff reached for a beer from his refrigerator. There was leftover pizza warming in the microwave, and the combination of the two is what he had looked forward to after working outside in the heat. He turned on the TV in hopes of capturing updates of his handy work. He was surprised how no media had yet reported how the attorney general died. The other occupants were expendable, collateral damage; and he rationalized how they got what they deserved hanging around corrupt politicians. He calculated he would most certainly be seen sitting alone in the borrowed truck, but he had not. He was prepared to handle any Good Samaritan who might have stopped by to lend a hand. Other loose ends were also in his cross hairs. The unsuspecting truck owner had no idea of his unfortunate fate if the truck had been seen and the license plate identified. He was expecting to see police cars en route to or from the Lincoln landmark. He hadn't seen anyone, and he was confident that their trail was cold before the fire was extinguished. He was right.

He knew he was finally making a name for himself. He was doing something everyone else just talked about. What he was doing made a difference and a statement to those who refused to listen to rational thinking, so he thought. However, frustration was becoming unbearable. Nobody was talking about him; not by name of course, but in generalities. All the news should be broadcasting who could do such a dastardly act or why would somebody do such a thing? People could at least know the wreck was no accident. It was well-orchestrated, and he was a true Patriot. Crooked politicians should be removed from office to let honest people govern. Somebody should at least be talking about why he did what he did.

They should be intelligent enough to figure out that part. The media could not be trusted. What he was witnessing was truly fake news. It appalled him when people would believe what they reported. He was beginning to believe more must be done to open the eyes of the naysayers.

At least his mom would suspect it was him, if only she had even heard about it. He often thought about his mom, how she was doing or even if she ever thought about him. He had grown up without a father and had to learn the meaning of responsibility at a very young age. At an early age his mom explained how little boys like him never had a dad. It was at that impressionable age he learned he had to be the dad he never had. It was his responsibility to get his own meals and do house chores until she came home from work. When she got laid off from the grocery store, things changed dramatically. He dropped out of high school to get a job. All the state assistance she applied for just was not enough. After she was caught multiple times for shoplifting, he learned he was old enough to be on his own. He quit staying with friends because the house rules were never his thing. His mother quit writing him. Before long, he learned she was in a female prison for her continued shoplifting practices.

He hated how the state of Kentucky had discarded him like trash. The government blamed the people who were having hard times as a product of their own doing. Politicians ruin the economy with their feel-good policies and then blame the people for not doing their part when businesses close or move elsewhere. Ruben remembered when the governor, at that time, was not re-elected for a second term. The Kentucky attorney general race was uncontested. The A.G. swore he would save the state millions and put people to work. He closed safe houses for youth who had no support system. While in office, he lobbied for the reduction of funding for foster care programs. He forced responsible adults to withdraw from becoming foster parents. Ruben had a deep, vile hatred for him and never forgave him for prosecuting his mom. She had no choice but to support him by whatever means necessary. The attorney general saw it differently, and Ruben was sure he had done the same to other kids, who found themselves in the same predicament. Ruben knew things would be worse if he were governor.

He heard his apartment door unlock, open, and then close. He knew Lex would be asking if there were any new updates from Kentucky. Ruben and Lex both came to their modest apartment after a day's work at about the same time. Lex was hired at the landscaping and lawn company where Ruben worked two weeks after Ruben was hired. They became part of a thriving business. They both had a multitude of previous jobs, but had not found anyone they worked with who had similar viewpoints. It made for long, unbearable work days. Now, they did not have to keep their viewpoints to themselves. They could pretty much talk about things freely and within earshot of others. Before Lex came to work there, Ruben reluctantly tried to engage in questionable conversation with coworkers on matters of government. It was clear to him, some didn't have his same viewpoint. Ruben needed employment, and losing another job due to coworker complaints would be unfathomable.

To save on expenses, they went fifty-fifty on all the bills. They rarely disagreed on anything, especially when it came to social and economic issues. They hated what was happening to their country and how political correctness was hurting hard-working people like themselves. They found growing sentiments on social media networks and decided between the two of them that more had to be done. They were boasting on networks about how the Patriots' message was delivered loud and clear. They weren't sure who exactly was listening, but they were reassured a lot of people felt the same way they did.

They agreed things went just like they had planned; but they were not happy about nobody knowing it was, in fact, a planned attack. The contiguous states of Kentucky were sending delegations to the memorial services for the attorney general. The Missouri governor delivered a statement from the desk of his office, flanked by the U.S. flag, the Missouri flag, and the Kentucky state flag. The Kentucky flag was centered between the other two with black ribbons draping from the top of the pole, signifying the state in mourning.

Ruben and Lex were infuriated by the Missouri governor's remarks. They could not believe he would care about a political party that was in contrast of his own, especially as conservative as he proudly claimed he was. Lex began ranting on social networks about Missouri not listening or understanding the peoples' voices – those who put him in office. Ruben was just as perplexed and livid as he, too, began his inciting opinions of those with like minds. They fed off each other's dislike of government and were pleased by the responses received through the networks.

"I'm a little surprised he even mentioned that he got our letter," said Ruben. "No other pea brain even acknowledged theirs."

"We can't be certain they did. Some trailer trash probably opened it and shredded the letter without it even getting to their governor's desk."

"We know Missouri got theirs. He was just stupid enough to admit it and tell everyone he's not going anywhere," Ruben continued.

"How do you know he was talking about your letter?"

"Our letter," Ruben corrected him. "The timing is right, and he might as well have been looking in your eyes when he said it."

"Well then. It's time Missouri understood what Kentucky feels like. This time they will know, it's not an accident," Lex said with a vile tone.

"Not just them, but the whole world will know Sovereign Citizen Patriots are what this country needs."

CHAPTER 12

Megan was already at the gym when Chad arrived. She was beginning to think this would be one of those days where she would be there, and he wouldn't. She thought about how she would approach him and perhaps see if he wouldn't mind helping her with strength exercises. She had already worked up a sweat on the treadmill and was cooling down when she saw him enter.

He headed to the weights and began his warm up when she came over to say hello. She was not shy at all. She grabbed one of the provided gym hand towels and slung it over her shoulder.

"Hello, it's Chad, right?"

"Hi, yes, it's Chad. How are you doing?"

"Just fine, thank you. You don't remember my name, do you?"

"Megan, right?"

"That's right. You do remember. I wasn't sure; we only met a few days ago."

"Trust me. I wouldn't have forgotten your name. So, how's your workout?"

"Just started my upper body. I was hoping you wouldn't mind helping me. You kind of implied when we met that you'd be willing to give me some pointers."

"No problem. Let me finish my warm ups, and I'll get with you."

The workout took longer than normal for them both. Chad helped with each exercise in between his own, all the while explaining form and technique. Megan took it all in and was appreciative of all she was learning. Fitness training had changed immensely since high school. She was pleased to have Chad offer to work with her. He had no issues with keeping things professional. He was on task and knew he would have to get straight to matters at hand as soon as possible. They ended their last reps and realized the workout was much longer than either normally stayed at the gym.

"Thanks for your help. I once thought about getting a trainer. Now I know it would be money well spent."

"No problem. Save your money though. I'll work with you when I can."

"Thanks, I may take you up on that. I think I'll take a quick shower and hit a drive-through somewhere. I've worked up an appetite," Megan smiled as she wiped sweat from her brow.

"Me, too. Sorry I kept you longer than normal. Want to grab a bite somewhere?"

"Sure, give me fifteen minutes," she replied.

Megan was hoping she would get an invite somewhere. She had a history where guys were oblivious to offers of open invitations. They drove a short two and one-half miles to a Panera across from the Battlefield Mall. The crowd was surprisingly thin, since it was mid-week. They both chose from the "Pick-Two" menu items. Chad sat at an open table strategically facing Battlefield Boulevard traffic and the entrance door. The few patrons dining were varied. There were the young and carefree, giggling between themselves, while looking at apparent photos on each other's cell phones. There were the mature couples who seemed annoyed at the constant giggling of the young girls, all the while wishing they could view what was so funny about the pictures. There were three others oblivious to all surroundings utilizing the free Wi-Fi. They appeared to be students working on projects, taking advantage of quieter surroundings than what they were probably accustomed.

"Thanks again for working with me today. You have no idea how much I appreciate it. I've been lax with my exercise, and I'm afraid it's beginning to show."

"You should tone it down somewhat on your two-a-days. That's how injuries occur," Chad warned. "Let your body recover."

"It's been two-a-days, but trust me, they haven't been hard. I'm not that dedicated."

Chad was trying to come up with the obvious questions but knew it was smart to let things just happen. He had to leave it up to her. They discussed more of how keeping an exercise routine simple helped the body stay toned and strong. They both agreed cardio and full-body strength routines were a required lifestyle if you wanted to live a long and healthy life. They discussed education, health marketing through insurance companies, governmental health initiatives, and how the U.S. remains among the highest in the world in obesity rates. They talked about public health trends in adults and youth. It was clear they both could hold an intelligent conversation regarding health, and it was an enjoyable discussion about several matters of interest to them both. Then she asked the obvious question he was waiting for.

"So, what do you do?'

"I'm a consultant for a private security firm."

"That's sounds interesting. Securities as in money market and investments or security as in, if you tell me you'll have to kill me."

They both smiled, and Chad noticed the extended stare into his eyes. She was very pretty, and her chosen fragrance permeating around them was seductive.

"The latter," Chad countered with another smile.

"Oh my, sounds intriguing. Seriously, what do you do?"

"I am serious. I consult for a security organization. I got in during the company start up, and I've been there ever since."

"What's the name of the company? Let me guess, if you tell me …"

"Sort of but not really. It's private and not public record. I don't plan on …"

"OK, now you've got my curiosity up. You can't tell me the name, and it's not public knowledge. It's not like I know what a narc looks like, and I suppose that's the point. But you don't look like a narc."

"I work for a firm within Homeland Security. They're looking for someone who is talented. If you're interested, I can see what I can do."

"Oh, I'm interested. How could I not be with that tease?"

CHAPTER 13

Ruben and Lex were up until the early morning hours fueling the fire and getting refueled from social media outlets, militia and Patriot web sites. They could sleep in and knew they could have stayed up all night relating how the out-of-control, big government was ruining lives.

Their lawn mowing work rotation had them both off for the next week at least. No forecast of rain, which normally had them working shorter rotations. The competition of new landscaping contracts with new home and business construction, was fierce. The company they worked for had nothing that would keep them overly busy, and they looked forward to staying out of the intense summer heat.

Lex was having his morning coffee, although it was almost noon.

"There's not much coffee. You want me to make another pot?" asked Lex.

"Nah, that's alright; I'll get it."

"Did you see all that stuff from the student last night?" Lex asked.

"Yeah, I did. I'm trying to figure out if he was for real or just another one of those all talk and no action guys."

"He sounded legit. It wouldn't be too hard to check up on him."

"I'm not sure about that. Whoever you call could just say it's policy, and they only release information upon written request."

"He could be an asset for us."

"I agree, an expendable asset," Ruben said, with that familiar sour tone in his voice. "He is kind of over the top. He really hates the feds because they supposedly got him expelled from school."

"I saw online what you're talking about. He said something about cops getting a tip about him dealing drugs, and the feds made it stick even though nothing was found."

Ruben admitted, "He's ripe for the pickings that's for sure."

"Dude, you're saying you want to put him to work?"

"Why not and why not now? I'm tired of what is happening around us. This guy is obviously a Patriot at heart. Let's get in his head and see if he has any bite to that bark of his."

Ruben and Lex both got online to chat about a revolution, and how they benefit people who are suppressed. All respondents were adamant about change, but nobody had any clue about what they were proposing. A little prodding and intellectual correspondence all but silenced chat forums. No one understood what was being said, and interjecting proved the point. Most didn't understand politics, economy, social injustice or how they all related to each other.

Ruben knew they wouldn't be the leaders of any revolution. He and Lex had other missions in mind, and they were ready to battle anyone who were traitors of the Constitution. Every time a politician would take to the airways and preach freedom and democracy, a nauseous feeling would come over him.

They talked the good talk, but on day two after being elected or reelected, they were already asking for more money for their next election campaign. All too soon, they were forgetting the people who put them in power. Then their coffers would overrun while passing menial legislation. If anything worthwhile passed, it was because of the heavy donors who bought their vote. The vicious cycle continued while they promised to increase education funding and lower taxes.

Ruben had the stronger personality of the duo. Lex followed his methods of thought, but they disagreed often on what should be done about it. Lex was more of a doer, without the consequences type of mentality. He would worry about the "what if" later. It had served him well all his life, but after working alongside Ruben, he understood more of the intellectual method of accomplishing what needed to be done. He had a hard time taking that stance. When Ruben became obsessed with the attorney general, he understood more about the ways and means. It had not bothered him one bit becoming involved in defending the people's rights by whatever means necessary. He was looking forward to doing something positive for all the Patriots who did not have the means.

It was that immature enthusiasm that got the attention of the D.C. analysts. The tweet made by Lex fueled more followers, but it was his lack of restraint that infuriated Ruben. Lex was certain he would not make that mistake again. He had seen Ruben's temper flare many times, and the threatening of his own life, he wouldn't soon forget. However, both were unaware they were in the cross hairs and were being hunted.

Lex felt like he was an innocent bystander when the A.G. was taken out. Ruben's strong personality made sure he knew he, too, was expendable. Lex never forgot what Ruben told him when he doubted the success of what they were trying to pull off.

"I will do the will of the Patriots, with or without you. You'll get on board, or you'll not see another birthday."

Media did not follow the social network venues Ruben and Lex had become intimately familiar with. If they had, they, too, would have put the timeline together about the Kentucky basketball team and the so-called accident. It had barely hit the news wires when Lex sent out his snide joke in an online forum. Ruben vowed not to go to prison and would fight to the death to keep the cause alive. Lex learned at that moment of their one-sided discussion who would be boss.

Ruben was committed to fighting for all Patriots and that meant even to the death. Lex knew things could be just as easy as their last mission. With timing and preparation, things would go smoothly. He was not worried and didn't understand why Ruben had any concerns. However, Ruben's suggestion of taking on another Patriot to join them could be risky. Particularly, if the real reason he was forced to leave his school was due to drug usage. Taking on a drug addict would be cause for concern and too risky for what they had at stake. He was sure Ruben was going to move on to the next constitutional threat to America's freedom and he could do nothing to stop him.

CHAPTER 14

They were a tandem couple during their strength training exercises. There was little talk about anything other than encouragement during each other's reps during their circuit training.

"I can't thank you enough for all your help. I, of course, normally go it alone," Megan said during a much-needed pause.

"It's my pleasure. I, too, go it alone; but, of course, I never was asked to help anyone before."

"That's rather hard to believe. If that's true, then you really must have felt sorry for me."

"Not at all. You're a natural. It's just important to keep good technique and form so as not to cause any injuries."

"I don't think I'll fire you just yet. I'm enjoying the company as I torture myself."

"So, I'm torturing you now? I may have to increase my fees, so you'll feel more like you're getting your money's worth."

"And I see how it is. You get me hooked, and then you raise your rates. Sounds like false advertising to me."

"Nothing false about it. What you see is what you get."

"It's the no pain, no gain training you're putting me through?" Megan smirked.

"Not at all. Besides, that's old school. You push your body to the limit to the point of muscle fatigue, but you don't injure yourself doing it."

"Got it. Leave here with a good workout but not dread returning because I'm still hurting from the last time I was here."

"Exactly."

"How about I meet you at Panera for tea after I shower. I'm intrigued about your possible hooking me up with a job; that is, if the offer's still standing."

"The offer still stands, and I'll spring for the tea."

Chad arrived first and sat with his iced tea watching the entryway for Megan. He was surprised to find the exact same table for two was open when they were there before. After about thirty minutes, he began to wonder about her delay in getting there. He remembered though he had showered quickly and arrived before her with the purpose of preparing his employment and consulting work talk. He hadn't prepared to talk about what he did or how everyone in MoTAF operated. He wasn't sure if she would even believe what he was telling her. He had to follow the plan and phase one was complete - they had met and were becoming friends.

He was a little anxious of how she might react to knowing exactly what he did. He had to approach it with caution. He had not been in this situation before and had planned just to let it evolve as she inquired and asked more.

He was focusing on the way the company came into existence and how he got involved with MoTAF. He noticed Megan approach the door and realized why she might have taken a little longer than expected. Her hair was curled, and she was wearing a sundress that flowed as she approached the entrance. She looked directly to where he was seated. She smiled in his direction, and he waved to her acknowledgement. She paid for her tea and made her way over to the table. Chad appreciated his view of the entrance as he watched those busily moving in and out of the restaurant. Different patrons were dining this time, although nearly twice as many people were present and were also diverse in age. It was a nice, calming atmosphere.

"I see you definitely got out of your gym attire," Chad said jokingly, as she pulled out her seat to join him.

She apologized for being late and then added, "I see you couldn't wait to buy my tea."

"Oh, I'm sorry. I did say I'd buy your tea."

"Yes you did, but I wouldn't have waited either. I ran by my house-- hope you didn't wait too long."

"I haven't had a refill yet, so that should tell you something."

"It's good to know you're one to pace yourself when you drink," she said with what seemed to be a flirtatious turn of her head.

Her long hair hung down freely and almost covered her face as she looked at him. He sat nearly straight in his chair with his right elbow on the table while grasping his glass of tea. Chad then crossed his legs sitting sideways at the table trying not to telegraph how uncomfortable and suddenly awkward he felt. A flirtatious aura surrounded him.

"So where did we leave off from the last time we were here?" she asked, reminding him of their varied conversation from before.

"I think we were at the social injustices crippling our country and why you thought we should continue spending billions of dollars to ensure the economy remains strong."

She jokingly and with a broad smile, made a fist placing it over her mouth while pretending she was choking.

"So, that's how you remember our conversation do you? I seem to recall it in distinct contrast to your memory. Maybe I should enlighten you."

Chad laughed while looking out the window at the traffic motoring by and of the pickup truck pulling into the restaurant parking. It didn't have a tailgate, and the rear license plate was bent beyond recognition as the driver parked, angling in facing away from Panera.

Megan noticed the smile that was once on his face had slightly diminished as she turned to look in the direction he was looking. She didn't see anything worth noting but noticed Chad was still looking out the window. She looked again to see what he was looking at.

"What's the matter?"

"That guy that pulled up in that truck is just sitting there and not getting out to come in. Maybe he's waiting on someone."

"Like you had to wait on me," she said, smiling at him in an apologetic way.

"Like I said, I had just gotten here not long before you.

She turned again noticing the truck Chad had seemed to focus on. She made a quick glance but turned back to drink her tea. She looked at Chad realizing his fixation was away from her and back in the direction of the truck. What she hadn't seen was the man sitting in the truck apparently talking--not on a phone or to someone in the truck, but to himself. Chad could see what appeared to be a frustrated individual. Megan noticed how

Chad's posture changed. He was no longer sitting with his legs crossed, and he was pushing his chair back and starting to stand. He was staring out the window while moving all in one motion.

"Leave your tea; we have to go," Chad said as he reached with his left hand helping her stand.

Megan turned to see what he was looking at. She barely turned around when she was grabbed around her waist forcing her to move toward the rear seating area. His hand was firm at her waist, and she was being forced where he wanted her to walk. She tried to glance back but was startled by being handled abruptly and without her approval. Chad was looking in the direction of where they were seated. That's when she saw the gun Chad was holding in his right hand.

He saw the man exit his truck, appearing to slam his door shut and walk toward the restaurant entrance with a long-barreled gun. They were nearing the emergency exit when the loud booms rang out. Simultaneously, people started screaming. She knew exactly what it was and where it was coming from. They both lowered their heads as glass could be heard shattering. She hit the emergency exit with both hands and heard the loud obnoxious emergency exit alarm as they cleared the door. The gunshots continued as screams could be heard over all else. She felt the touch of Chad's hand on the small of her back as she instinctively ran to the closest car in the lot while shielding herself from the building. She looked back at the restaurant, noticing Chad holding what looked like her GLOCK 27. "Let's move to my car," he said as they both noticed a pause in the gun shots.

"Hold on, he may be coming back out," she said as they looked toward both exit doors.

People were screaming and running, getting distance between them and the shooter. They were still exiting, several falling over others, as they ran out of the restaurant. Chad was now in front of Megan, making their way down the row of angled parked cars. She didn't know what he drove, but Chad had his keys in his left hand pressing the remote. Megan realized which car was his by the deafening car horn sounding as they approached. She threw open the driver side rear door and climbed in without saying a word as Chad got behind the wheel. He almost struck a young girl running across the lot as he was backing up. He had remembered her from inside the restaurant. There were a good number of people inside, and he hoped they all were able to get out, although he was afraid the wounded or killed count could be huge. He pulled out of the lot and into an adjacent parking lot before trying to exit onto Battlefield Boulevard. There was a lull in traffic, and he accelerated quickly, all the while glancing into his rear-view mirror. He could not see Megan but knew she was prone either on the floor or on the rear seat.

"We're clear," he shouted. "You can sit up now."

"We've got to call the police!" Megan said loudly as if it would be difficult being heard from the rear seat.

"Don't bother. Almost everyone running from inside had a phone to their ear. I'm just glad I didn't run over any of them."

"But what if they're all calling their loved ones to tell them what happened and not the police."

She had a point and Chad knew it. He was trying to navigate through traffic quickly and safely, all the while trying to unlock his screen on his phone. "Never mind, slow down, and I'll call them myself."

They both could hear sirens at the same time but couldn't tell where they were coming from. As they approached another intersection, they could see oncoming flashing headlights as well as red and blue lights approaching them. They noticed the same flashing lights coming from another direction. Chad slowed down and pulled to a stop, as did others who had come to the intersection. The steady green light was yielding for Chad's direction, but no one moved into the intersection. All approaching emergency police cars were like a caravan headed in the same direction. It was obvious to them where they were going. They realized they were probably the only ones at that intersection who knew what had just happened.

"How did we get this far from Panera? I don't remember us getting this far. Slow down. I don't want you to accidently shoot me while trying to drive."

"Trust me; you're in good hands."

"I think I can trust you. But you have to admit, we just met not too long ago, and I don't know anything about you."

"Agreed. I think that's what I was getting to when all hell broke loose."

"Perhaps we can continue another day, but let's not do Panera. I'm done with the "Pick-Two" menu," Megan said as she tried to compose her appearance while in the rear seat.

They looked at each other through the rearview mirror simultaneously knowing there was nothing funny about what was occurring at the restaurant.

"Where exactly did you park your car? It could be in the middle of a crime scene."

"Oh, crap! I hadn't thought about that. I came up National and pulled into that Quicken Loans parking lot. I didn't think there would be any spots open, although there were a few."

"We should be fine. Let's come in from National like you did and see how close we can get. You may have to come back and get it later."

They pulled into the Quicken Loans lot, all the while noticing the abundance of law enforcement presence from afar. They both scanned the adjacent parking lot, trying to see what more was occurring. They noticed the traffic was backing up at different side streets as they approached from the rear. Yellow police tape had already been roped around the complete parking area surrounding the Panera. Flashing red and blue lights remained activated from parked police cruisers. There were several SUV's with flashing emergency lights as well. They, too, appeared to be police vehicles mainly because of the multiple antennae on the roofs. Chad pulled into the adjacent parking lot and was directed to pull near a modest SUV. Both were sucked into the scene like a vacuum not wanting to look away. They were not the only ones. People started gathering to the roped-off areas with anticipation of finding out what had occurred. An ambulance and fire truck were blocking all available areas of maneuvering in and out of the Panera lot. There were not going to be any vehicles arriving or leaving there anytime soon.

"Guess I'll see you at the gym," Megan said as she climbed, un-ladylike out of the rear seat.

"I guess so. It'll be interesting to see what the news has to say about what happened today."

"I know I'll be watching," Megan said.

"Hold on a second," Chad replied as he got out of his car while watching the scene unfold at Panera. "Let me give you my number. I'm not sure if I'll be at the gym tomorrow as early as I normally do."

She entered the number in her phone. "Let me give you mine, so you'll have it, too."

"You don't have to give me yours, if you don't want to," Chad assured her.

"I want you to have it. You may want to call me, as well, sometime."

She dialed the number he just gave her and waited a few seconds for Chad's response.

"Got it, thanks," he looked at his phone as he added her number to his cell's address book. "I'll talk to you soon."

"OK, thanks. By the way, thanks for watching out for me," she turned and got into her car before he could respond. They followed each other from the parking lot all the while dodging onlookers.

CHAPTER 15

The services for the attorney general were lining up to be a huge political event. The Patriot Ryders motorcyclists were lining the street outside the cathedral. It was apparent the Westboro Baptist Church had made the trip from Topeka, Kansas. Although their numbers were small in attendance, the signs they held were proclaiming the untimely death, was at the hands of the general's own doing. U.S. flags were flowing majestically, being held firmly by the hands of the Patriot Ryders on both sides of the roadway.

Ruben adjusted his headset. He was standing alongside countless other mourners who lined the street outside the Frankfort Cathedral. He had a ringside seat of the funeral procession as it would leave the church. Lex stood solemnly with others barely a block away listening through his headset as well. The crowd was dense, but they knew where each other stood. They had counted the light poles and were standing strategically from each other and on opposite sides of the street behind the rows of U.S. flags, held by the motorcyclists and rows of people. Neither of them had anticipated the show of support from the Ryders. Neither of them liked the thought of challenging them either. Even the women with their leather jackets with Harley emblems were a force to be reckoned with. Many were proudly displaying rocker panels on the backs of their jackets. The respected group was from all over, especially Kentucky and Missouri. There wouldn't be another profound statement from Sovereign Citizen Patriots today.

Ruben knew Lex was listening. They had been talking openly to each other, maneuvering through the crowd to get to their predesignated viewpoints.

"I'm calling off our assistant. Whatever he planned will not work. Too many cops."

Ruben cuffed his hand over his mouth to help eliminate others hearing what he was saying.

"Roger that." Lex kept his vantage point because he wanted to see what everyone else had come to see.

Lex knew the newly-chosen Citizen Patriot would be a liability if he tried something. Ruben's decision to use this kid wasn't very smart. How could they know if he could be trusted? He had not seen this much show of force in one place before, and it was unsettling. It also infuriated him.

Ruben hadn't caused anyone to be uneasy with his presence. No one paid any attention to him when he spoke into his mike. He had proven to be such an ally with those standing around him. He was almost showing tears of how unfortunate all this had been and praised the work of the attorney general. He was almost to the point of overkill with his praise and realized he had to tone it down, or there would be doubters around him. He was enjoying the fruits of his labor.

He picked up his burner phone and dialed the student's burner cell number. It rang several times before it was answered. "Hello."

"Where are you? You need to stand down. Whatever it is, stand down."

Ruben was normally cautious. He felt he was a little off his game from the taunting he was doing with the onlookers.

"Did you hear me? I said stand down."

The recording of the phone conversation was activated upon the first ring. Everyone in the room was listening intently to the voice on the other end. The rented room at the hotel was packed. A conference room table with plush armrest chairs were scattered around the room. The air conditioning was turned down, but it was barely comfortable. The body heat along with the electronic equipment made it clammy and close. A sign attached to the exterior of the closed door kept out curious onlookers. Capital letters depicting an acronym of a boring organization business meeting was in progress. Even those inside the room wondered who came up with the letters, which meant absolutely nothing. There were analysts furiously noting everything on laptops. Keystrokes were sounding off like rain in a thunderstorm on a tin roof. There were barely enough electrical outlets for all the power needed to perform the tasks at hand. The room went suddenly silent. Everyone was listening intently to catch every word and sound of the conversation being recorded.

"I'm here. Why stand down? I can barely hear you. Why should I stand down?" All keystrokes had stopped. Everyone was waiting for the callers' response. A triangulation of the call couldn't be pinpointed. The burner phones left little to no tracing codes.

"There's too much security. It's not worth the risk."

"I'm the one taking the risk," said a voice with a static unclear crackle. "You just stand back and watch the show."

The analyst was doing his best recording and forwarding the conversation, while getting as much information about whom he was talking with and what his plans were. The analyst was observant to the sounds or the lack of sounds coming from the recording. There was no recognizable background noise during segments of conversation. No moving train sounds, bells ringing from storefront enticements, or horns blown from lake or riverfronts, no whistles blown from intersection traffic cops. Analysts in the room were cupping hands over their headsets as if to get better sound clarification.

"If you don't want to get caught, we can do this another time and on a bigger stage," Ruben ordered.

"There is no bigger stage than the one you're on right now. Join me, and we can both watch the show together."

Ruben closed the flip phone. He knew he had to cut his losses before there were gains. The call just didn't seem right. He couldn't put his finger on it, but why would a kid risk being caught. Patriot or not, youth do not rationalize like this kid. Nothing could be traced to him, but he couldn't get careless no matter what was at stake. He sounded just like he appeared in his blog and networking conversations. Ruben was enjoying the experience, but the excitement was waning, which made him nervous. Ruben didn't get nervous; he got personal retribution.

Brody was taken into custody on the way back to his Ford Bronco. He was trying to find a high vantage point. He was seen in several parking garages, asking questions about the memorial route to be taken for the attorney general. He got the attention of local police from his varied movements and questions he was asking people. He was observed entering apartment buildings and roaming stair wells. It was determined, when talking to people, he did not live in those dwellings. The local police took notice when they had received several calls with the description of the same young male attempting to enter an office building without a proximity access card. It was reported he told someone who refused to let him enter that he forgot his card when in fact the person worked at that office for years and had not ever seen him before. When he was approached by law enforcement, he became defensive. It was obvious he didn't care much for their intrusion.

Analysts were hitting keystrokes as soon as the cell connection ended. Face recognition scanning could not work with any certainty. The crowds were too thick and mobile. The voice recognition program was coming up with nothing. All efforts were beginning to look like a bust. Every signal-controlled intersection with a video system was operational and being monitored from the conference room. Nothing worth noting was observed. Social media appeared to be nonexistent regarding the services. It was like nobody cared. The number of people who came out to view the processional was something to see. It was perhaps the most publicized event of the year. A lot of people supported the attorney general, or at least his ideals.

Homeland Security friends were dressed in the all-familiar attire. It was a small interrogation room in the back of a county sheriff's department. A young college student was no longer smug or brazen. Three men in black suits looked at a file and told the young man what he already knew. He had no one in his family who claimed him. He was a loner. The insurance money from a great-grandparent was nearly gone. It was the money willed to him after he convinced them he needed help in a get-rich scheme. It was too late when the family found out about it, and no lawyer would take the case to prosecute. He was on his own. What money he did have could soon belong to the federal government. The young man was learning the hard way. The Patriot Act was what would educate him in a different learning institution. Brody gave it one last shot to call their bluff.

"I want to call my lawyer," he demanded. "I have constitutional rights that are afforded every U.S. citizen."

One of the men in a dark suit said in a professional business-like tone,

"Brody, next time you should know who you team up with. The U.S. doesn't afford the same rights to terrorists--at least not for several months. Maybe a lawyer won't mind ruining his career and taking your case."

Another man in the room, who appeared to be wearing the same dark suit, chimed in, "It's time to go. There are some new classmates who you'll want to meet at your new school. It's a short ride to the Kentucky Federal Correctional University."

"He's smarter than that," a suited guy looked at another as if he was not in the room. "He's not taking the fall for something he couldn't get done." He looked back at Brody again. "Your friend is letting you take the fall. Think about what's happening here."

Brody sat in the uncomfortable metal chair squirming. He was now believing that he would be taken away and not missed by anyone. He was a loner, and he knew it. He could not believe he was again surrounded by cops who were ruining his life. He was trying to think fast and decided a lawyer, any lawyer, would put an end to this nonsense.

"I want my lawyer. I know my rights. We're done here."

The men chuckled out loud and looked at each other, and one of them said, "I think you need to pinch yourself. This is not a dream."

"I thought you were smart," said another man leaning over the hard-surfaced wooden table. "Didn't you understand what we read to you regarding the Patriot Act? There will be no lawyer until we say you get one."

"Obviously, he's been sleeping in class," said a dark suited man.

"You're going to have a lot of time to study for your next exam," another chimed in.

"What do you want from me? I didn't do anything," Brody asked.

"Exactly. Just like you didn't do anything on your previous college campus. How'd that work out for you?"

"I didn't do anything. You guys got me suspended, and now they say I owe them tuition."

"I think he's starting to learn something here. This study group is going to work out just fine."

An analyst from MoTAF was talking to one of their federal assistants who was aiding in the interview. He was observing the interview behind the dark tinted glass pane. The young student was obviously there to administer deadly force but never got to the point of committing the act.

There was nothing tangible to tie him to any act, only speculation. After the call was concluded, the analyst sounded dejected, like he had just found out he lost his dream job. The job he had prepared himself by putting all his eggs in one single basket.

"So far it's a bust with the student. He didn't know who he was helping. They've got him under the Patriot Act, so they can hold him for a while. They're still working on him, but it doesn't look promising."

"Let's try to turn him," chimed another analyst. "See if the bad guys will pick up and talk to him again. It's worth a try."

After several minutes of discussion, they came up with which conversation ploy to use. They had to make direct contact with the so-called Patriots. Some professional coercion had to be implemented. Nothing like water boarding, but just as effective. The small statured young student wasn't a match for the burly, suited men.

"Sorry about that," one of the men said smugly, as they let loose of the choke hold they had placed on him. "I think you'll be just fine. They tested this stuff in rats and they performed just like they were expected to."

Brody didn't particularly appreciate the injection at the back of his jaw line just below his left ear. He knowingly agreed to work with them but couldn't explain the mind-altering decision he just made. At that very moment, he was more determined to get out of his predicament at any cost. He was painfully aware of agreeing to something he had previously been protesting.

Another suited man continued, "You'll be a little nauseated for a while and have a slight headache, but you'll be fine. You'll later feel like you're recovering from a drunken stupor with the worst hangover you've ever had."

The other man smiled big and asked if he was ready to talk to his friend. He looked at the men, one at a time, as if each gaze was in playback filmography slow motion.

"You guys are enjoying this way too much. Perhaps you should think about securing different employment."

He was convinced to cooperate and was wanting to assist with all kinds of enthusiasm. It felt uncharacteristic and extremely odd. He knew whatever was in his system would have him making all kinds of wrong decisions. They convinced him to talk to the voice on the other end, the man who he communicated with online. He was their link to stopping the Patriots. They knew the path they needed to take; they just weren't sure where that path was taking them. The men in suits dialed Ruben's number with the interface tracing software, put it on speaker, and handed the phone back to Brody.

Ruben looked down at the cell number as it chimed in his hand. "Yeah, what?"

"You're right, I should wait. Let's meet so we can decide how to do this."

The analysts looked around the room as everyone waited to record every spoken word. Ruben dropped the cell in the nearest trash can. The line went dead as he headed to the pre-established rendezvous and waited for Lex.

CHAPTER 16

The room was deafeningly silent. All the analysts were hoping for some sign, some clue, some type of mistake the call would have presented. There was too much unrecognizable background noise to determine where he was. They had tried previously, when Ruben was talking to Lex. They muffled-out the voices and other ambient sounds in hopes of pinpointing a location. They weren't ready to pull the plug just yet.

He was a fish out of water and knew it. He was not from the area, and due to his questionable actions, he found himself surrounded once again by men in uniform. Like any clandestine operation, a command post was set up to organize and manage anything that could possibly occur. The analysts received intelligence from their local contact and were informed about a person of interest. Once he was located, the local police were more than happy to turn things over to Homeland Security. There would be no more nuisance calls about him the rest of the day.

Again, Brody was met by men in dark suits. He didn't recognize their faces because they were not the same people from before; but he knew of them, and the games they liked to play. Everyone had a profile picture of him. He had not changed any in such a short time, but he was making a name for himself. Nobody, other than analysts, called him by his birth name. "Kid" sounded more appropriate. He was now making an impression on those who had not met him. His brazen rhetoric was only seen in his online chats and blogs. Not until now had he been taken seriously. He had joined allegiances with obvious terrorists and was fast becoming a serious foe. Those of MoTAF understood Brody was dangerous and should be treated accordingly.

He openly admitted there was a rifle in a padded carrying case in his Bronco. It was his right to have it, and he had not threatened anyone or been seen doing anything with it. He was smug until he found out he was not going home. He was dumb enough to allow himself to be located so easily. When he boasted online about Missouri being next for a memorial service, he marked himself. He came to realize that the game he was playing, he may have already lost. Things had turned for the better when he started seeing things their way. He was in these same circumstances, once again, he realized he couldn't win – not in the long scheme of things. He was coming around, and it looked like he was going to play like a ball in a pinball game. He had turned 180 degrees and was going to roll over on the Patriots.

It was explained how he could remain a productive citizen, or he could become a statistic in the penal system and not be heard from for a very long time. He could end his life on his own terms, if he failed to help them. They read to him part of the U.S. Patriot Act once again, which got him to understand his need to reverse the chain of events to which he had become involved. He was learning more than any classroom instruction he had ever received.

Brody explained it was an online chat forum, and he could not tell who sent him the phone. He was surprised he received it. A typed note told him to call a number and encouraged him to be the Patriot everyone else was not ready to be. He did not think he would get anything in the mail and did not expect any package to arrive for him. He admitted attending the funeral of the attorney general but still denied wanting to harm anyone. He stated he was wanting a high vantage location but was not there to harm anyone. It was understood he did not commit the act, but he could be charged, convicted, and incarcerated for what he had already admitted. It was the impact of his actions, not the intent of what he told them. He would assist the U.S. government in stopping the next assassination attempt.

He vehemently hated any form of state or federal government. It was not a position he would have ever thought he would have found himself. He was now working for the government and agreeing to do so. He was rolling over on somebody he had not met but praised. He admittedly was drawn to those who spoke similar philosophies and still aligned on more fronts than his friends in suits wanted to hear.

It was agreed. He would get in the good graces of his unknown friend and try to form a bond and create a meaningful scenario where they could eventually meet. He would be actively involved in what was to happen in Missouri.

Chad couldn't believe what he was hearing. A crazed right-wing nut case would be helping them stop whatever was being planned to happen in his home state. This was a first, and he was not sure this was going to be a positive outcome.

In the close-quartered room, Chad spoke up first. "Maybe we can check with FedEx and perhaps get a name and address of who sent the burner to Brody."

"Already done," said the Kentucky analyst. "It was purchased through the Internet from a foreign vendor. They don't care who made the order, only that the funds for the purchase covered all costs," he explained. The funding source was searched to no avail. There were fraudulent or stolen identity theft issues with the purchasing and ordering of the phone for Brody. It even appeared a third party was possibly involved. The phone was mailed to a bogus address, and then a forwarding address was amended to the bogus one where Brody received it.

"We're missing something here," Chad stared at his terminal. "It's obvious this isn't the first time he's done something like this. We need to think outside the box. That's what we do best."

"I think he made us. He didn't respond at all to our return call," the Kentucky analyst looked dejected. It was as if he was taking it personally. "There's no way we can get anyone inside the Patriots in time. We've got to locate this Ruben."

"Never say never," Chad spoke with confidence. "We'll create more anonymous online sympathizers. This guy may be smart, but he can't help but want his ego stroked. We'll catch him and all the other Patriots."

"I'm with you and so is everyone else in this room. But we've got to be honest with ourselves," concurred another analyst. "We have no idea how many Patriots are out there,"

"True, but I know how good we are," Chad boldly claimed. "They're careless, or we wouldn't be here right now."

"I'm with you," agreed the Kentucky analyst. "Brody is scared. He may be bold, but he realizes life as he knows it, no longer exists. We did well today. Nothing happened, and we have an 'in' with what's being planned next."

"That's right, this Kid is right where we want him to be." Chad stood from his reclined chair. "Let's see where he's able to take us, and maybe we can get someone to play along and have a sting on Ruben."

"Agreed," replied an analyst from the other side of the room. "We've come this far. We might as well be sitting in the same room with them planning all this. It's just a matter of time, and they're done."

Chad excused himself from the room after announcing he had to return several messages he received. He looked at three text messages from Megan. He thought hard on what type of reply he would send. He found himself deleting and editing sentence after sentence. He read hers again and then once more. He wanted to mention the Panera shooter, but she hadn't even mentioned it in her texts. How had that affected her? What was her mental state?

"How's your day?" was her first text.

Then another one, thirty-five minutes later, "When you get a chance, let me know when you're free." Forty minutes later, "I may not make it to the gym today."

He realized he was over analyzing how to reply to her. He needed to talk to her and needed to have that in-depth conversation very soon.

"Sorry I haven't gotten back with you. I've been in a closed-door meeting all afternoon. When I get back in town, I'll get with you. I need to run something by you." He pressed "send."

Chad wanted her to know he was out of town. It was time to bring her into the circle. She needed to know more about what he did and her thoughts on becoming a partner with MoTAF.

His cell buzzed almost immediately. He was holding it in his hand and was already retracing his steps back to the conference room. It almost startled him.

"I just finished my run. No need to go to the gym when my trainer is away," a smiley face emoji finished the sentence.

Chad drafted an immediate reply. He couldn't delay, especially as quickly as the reply she had just sent.

"How are you? Were you able to sleep after what you went through?"

"You mean what we went through. Yes, I'm fine. What is it you want my opinion on?"

"It's kind of complicated. When I get back, we can find a different place to eat."

"Hmm, once again the mysterious one. I'm intrigued; a consultant who needs to be consulted," another smiley face with a large grin followed.

"Let's do dinner tomorrow. I want to know all about what was said in the news about Panera. I've been out of the loop."

Megan could guess with almost certainty where he was. There was more news footage of the Kentucky attorney general memorial services than anything else. She figured he was part of the security forces surrounding all the dignitaries who attended. She had no clue what he needed to talk to her about. She started with a few different thoughts in mind. She had hoped she did not let on just how intrigued she was. It was exciting that her fitness program was beginning to get interesting.

CHAPTER 17

"Chad, we got a break," an analyst stepped out of the meeting room finding Chad staring at his phone. "He's going to roll for us. We're back in the game."

"We were never out of the game," Chad smirked as he followed him back into the room to find a briefing going on via a computer link for video conferencing.

They were huddled around each other trying to get a good view of the interrogators. The interviewers were an odd trio. One young man, appeared to be not much older than a college kid himself; the other two appeared to be seasoned veterans of interrogation tactics. Both men resembled the storyline of a movie. There was dim lighting in a small room with a dark tinted one-way window on one wall. The older agent was dragging on a cigarette, ignoring the restricted smoking sign on the wall behind him, while smoke filled the room. It was obvious he wasn't complying with any regulations. It would make any person admit to any crime they were being questioned about just to get out of the room and to a smoke-free environment.

Everyone was intent on learning what the agents had to say. The agents didn't learn as much as they had hoped. Brody was a freelancer and was not part of any organized group. He was just a brazen anti-government enthusiast. His views were magnified through social media and blogs. He was obviously a follower and easily manipulated. Although he was smart, with an above average IQ, he was rather simple-minded when it came to logical thinking. He was planning to commit a serious crime without any forethought of consequences. It was apparent to the agents from the interrogation, Brody hadn't planned on how he was going to pull off an assassination or whom he was even wanting to target. He came clean to keep himself from being incarcerated for years to come, or worse. He learned more about the Patriot Act than he ever had dreamed or wanted to know or even cared about.

The agents gave Brody a laptop. The apps on the laptop were exactly like those on the one he owned. Everything on Brody's old computer was loaded onto the new one for him to use. There was one caveat with the new computer. It was easily traceable, and every keystroke could and would be tracked. Brody wasn't pleased with his new-found volunteer project. He found himself in a predicament that needed to right itself. He didn't know if there was any chance of righting the ship, but he was positive it was sinking and sinking fast.

The video camera on his new laptop would always be activated, even though it may not show as such in the computer settings. He had to continue with his blogging and social media contacts as if nothing had occurred prior to this day. If any settings were to change on his computer, he would find himself in some lock down facility, which no state jurisdiction would have ever heard of. He was to join or accompany any of his associates on any road trips like the one he had just taken with malicious or illegal intent. He was a smart young man, although cocky. He did understand he couldn't entice any activity of wrongdo   lue to entrapment laws. He was also intelligent enough to understand his life had been forever altered. He was a marked man by the very people he disliked. He saw no way out, and he was correct in his assumption.

"When will he contact the guy who was with him today?" asked Chad. "We need to catch these guys. Today was too close for comfort."

"He's going to start blogging again. We've also set him up with our smart phones. He was so pleased to join us – voluntarily, of course," the agent grinned as he elbowed his younger counterpart. "He understands any attempt to engage with social media or any multimedia contacts, other than through our devices, he forfeits all agreements with continuing his life as he previously knew it."

"What about these Sovereign Citizen Patriots?" another analyst asked. "What can you tell us about what we're up against?"

"Our so-called 'volunteer' knows little. He's pretty sure there are only those on blogs who have joined their movement as he calls it," the elder agent looked at his counterpart as if giving a nonverbal approval for him to speak.

"There are at least two others involved in the Kentucky crash," the young agent spoke with surprising confidence and authority. He seemed like he could be poised in a board room of powerful executives, and they all would be hanging on his every word.

"We are proceeding forward to seek approval for a signature strike," the agent continued. "We have enough dialogue through what they've communicated and as much as admitted to facilitating the traffic crash."

All the analysts were looking around at each other in amazement. This was a first. Something they had only heard about in acts of war occurring on foreign soil. No one wanted to ask anything further of the agents about the signature strike. Could they be talking about a drone strike or a precise clandestine assault? It was above their pay grade, and nobody wanted to get called out on that front.

A signature strike could come from any of the different federal departments. But it would have to be a cabinet head who approved such lethal action. Normally one reserved for the President, under these circumstances, a clandestine organization operating under the cloak of the federal government could function indefinitely. Plausible deniability could manifest a fine web of secrecy that could span over several departments. If one would try to unwind the web under the people's right-to-know clause, they would find themselves entering a deep, dark abyss that would span over several decades, if not more in search of the answers.

They all knew the agent was talking about the President of the United States, but nobody wanted to voice it. Maybe they were unilaterally using the phrase as an understanding that the head of Homeland Security, CIA or Pentagon commanders would use maximum force to eliminate another attack.

They knew there would be no loose ends following any such action. They were all on the same page, and domestic terrorism was what they were fighting. Their mission was absolute and resolute. The stakes were high, and the lines had already been crossed. The perpetrators were to be met with extreme prejudice. They only hoped they wouldn't be expecting or anticipating retaliation or any type of resistance. The threat needed to be eliminated and with stealth-like precision.

CHAPTER 18

Megan felt like a new person. Her morning run was a good start to her day. Right after her run, she was going to make an abbreviated workout at the gym. She had missed a day and thought it would be good to at least shorten her upper body workout. Trainer, or not, she had to keep up her routine even without guidance. It was ingrained in her since a young age and going without some form of physical exercise would be out of character. Now, however, it was a different kind of fun and with a different kind of purpose.

The text she received during her run was unexpected. Perhaps it was the message from Chad that gave her day a different kind of jumpstart. He knew she would be in her morning routine. He was rather specific in his message.

"Hey! Hope your run was a good one. I've got to wrap up some stuff before I get back. No need to reply, but let's grab dinner somewhere. Preferably where we can sit and look down at the menu. I'll get with you soon."

She didn't want to send a reply. If he was busy, it would be an annoyance just to let him know she got his message. Besides, he said there was no reason to reply. She was definitely looking forward to seeing him. She was enjoying his company but was painfully aware how business-like he remained from their first introduction. Although there seemed to be an obvious physical attraction, he didn't seem to make the obvious uncomfortable. She wanted to thank him for watching out for her during their lunch. Although he mentioned dinner, she was thinking she should be the one to buy as a "thank you".

Megan could not get over how sheltering he was during the active shooter. He was definitely a protector. What really intrigued her was his handling of his gun. How did she miss he was carrying one? She was unnerved by his frankness in getting her out of the restaurant, but was comforted in the way he was watching out for her. Even though she did not know him, it felt like he was protecting his mother or sister. It was an attraction about him that she couldn't deny, and there were several other things drawing her to him.

She confirmed her hair appointment and decided to treat herself to something new to wear. She felt deserving from the kind of day she was having; nothing more rewarding than a shopping trip to top off her brand-new self and have dinner with a new friend. She knew she had come a long way from hitting bottom. Her world was pulled out from under her like a magician quickly pulling a thin tablecloth from a table setting for four and not disturbing the wine glasses at each setting. She was sleeping better, and there were no nightmares from her unforgettable lunch. There were less frequent visits to the Springfield National Cemetery for remembrance and solitude. There were still conversations with her parents, but she would no longer linger at the cemetery where she would sit and spend countless hours.

The shopping wasn't as quick as she had hoped. There were so many looks she knew she could pull off, and she hadn't shopped for herself in a very long time. She started at Bath and Body. Wanting to find a new fragrance to accent her new look, she sought guidance to get the best possible deals for the money she wanted to spend. It wasn't but a short while, after talking to the store associate, that she realized she needn't worry about deals or specials. She was accustomed to asking for all the deals that weren't advertised or the overlooked online discount specials. There was so much she had to change about herself, and she liked her options. Kohl's was next on her list, then J. C. Penney's; she couldn't find the look she wanted. This dinner had to be special, but jotting all over town was going to dull the anticipation. She needed to decide what was going to be her look for dinner. A quick text to him would be a safe and wise decision if he was considering t-shirt and jeans. She willed against it. She felt childish with the thoughts of her not being decisive of what she was to wear. She wasn't sixteen.

Chad looked at his cell several times in hopes of receiving a message.

He didn't expect one, but none the less, he had hoped there was something to read from Megan Swift. He liked that name. It was becoming of her, and he found himself thinking of her a lot. He wasn't so sure it was all business, but he was sure it had to be kept that way. He was looking forward to getting back to familiar surroundings.

Brody came through, rolling over just when everyone thought it was a bust. There were moments when they thought they had to start at ground zero in hopes of finding the self-proclaimed terrorist. Their Patriot name was an offensive title they had given themselves. It made everyone even more determined to stop another attack. It was something they had all sworn to do, and they were excited about any involvement in preventing acts of terrorism.

Domestic terror had struck, and it was too close to home. They were confident another attack would be attempted, and this time it was to be in the "Show-Me State". According to all of the intelligence gathering, another threat in Kentucky was imminent, but with luck on their side, nothing would happen.

Chad was confident the intelligence would produce results, and they would prevent anything from happening in Missouri. However, he was also a realist. There are some things that just cannot be prevented. It is the level of the attempt, and the preparedness of the prevention that had Chad's level of awareness razor sharp. This is what they had been planning against, and he was going to do everything in his power, as well as everyone else, to avert whatever was being planned.

An update was provided to all the analysts prior to the command post dismantling. Brody was coming through on his promise. It was not like he had a choice, at least that is what they wanted him to think. A ruse was formulated about his being at the Kentucky services. Social media was buzzing, and it looked like Brody was back on point. He was getting multiple responses, and intelligence was surprised he could keep up with them all. Brody was being smart with his antics, and it seemed to be working. They were feeding off each other; everything was snowballing as anticipated. He could almost just sit back and view all ongoing comments about every form of government intrusion thinkable. It was like children on a playground deciding to play in the street instead of the safe confines of a fenced-in park with all the enticements every kid looked forward to.

CHAPTER 19

Megan Swift kept looking at her cell and the text Chad had just sent her. "Let's try the Flame at seven. Don't dress to impress, because I won't."

She was torn between what to wear. Should she have splurged a little more at the mall? What's the text supposed to mean? What was she to think? The last time she was at the Flame was for her prom. Several of the girls on her softball team decided to make a night of it and one to remember. Her dad gave her his credit card because he knew the tab would be more than she could endure. Her dad gladly paid for the tab for all four girls who were going to their prom together. Her eyes dampened as she recalled the night. Not because of the fun she had, but because her parents allowed her to have a memorable occasion. They had dined there several times before on many romantic evenings. Megan wasn't so sure she could accept the invitation. How could she go and not think of her parents? It could turn out to be a horrible time for Chad. A tear found its way down her right cheek. She glanced at the time on the DVD player's digital screen. She had just over three hours. Then, she realized it would be a thirty-minute drive downtown. She hadn't responded to his text. Megan felt tightness in her stomach and shortness of breath.

It was all starting to come back. There were two outs in the bottom of the ninth. The bases were loaded. She was up, and the opposing team had just switched pitchers. Their closer was now on the mound and was throwing warm ups. The loud smack of the ball hitting the catcher's mitt sent a nauseating churn to the pit of her stomach. It was up to her to win it or lose it. She still remembered the third baseman yelling, "Hey, batter, sucks to be you!" and how that almost caused her to pass out.

It was all coming back. Megan rose from her lounge position, while wiping the tears that found themselves now on both cheeks. She strutted to her bathroom to ready herself for showering. "I got this," she uttered out loud while recalling her line-drive double into the gap on the first pitch.

Chad was reviewing his talking points. He had rehearsed them in his mind several times over. He knew there would be questions, but he wasn't sure if she would want to hear the answers at that moment or even later after she could gather her thoughts. He could not anticipate how she would respond to what he was going to throw at her. The restaurant of choice was a way he could be assured of her undivided attention. The private setting would cause other concerns, but he was certain he could put a lid on it; at least, he hoped he could.

Others had expressed reservations about Megan being informed of MoTAF's purpose and mission. It was to the extent of trust and what could possibly happen if she questioned motives or even sided with certain opinions of opposing activists? Chad was prepared as much as he could be. Megan just had to show up and be willing to hear what he would propose. This was a first as was everything else so far. All MoTAF members were surprised that everything was still under the radar. The likelihood that domestic terrorism was successful would be a network rating goldmine. Then comes the opportunists relying on the fears of those who would empathize with the victims. People were already arming themselves at alarming rates around the country. It was paramount to eliminate any viable threats.

Chad's phone chimed with a short message, "See you there."

He sat at the bar viewing the entrance nearly an hour before their reservation time. He would have to explain the secluded seating and his leather business satchel, which occupied the stool next to him. She would wonder why he would bring work to a dinner date. He would get right to the point, if she pressed the matter. She had no idea this was a business meeting. He was sure she was assuming otherwise. There were multiple times she commented on his looks, or it was just the way she looked at him. She was near the point of being overly appreciative of his knowledge of physical fitness and his helping her as a trainer.

He was deep in thought of what he was going to say. Even as he watched the pedestrian traffic and occurrences, he missed her. He didn't recognize her at all. She had opened the door of the restaurant and was approaching the bar before he realized it was her. Her smile was practically a smirk. She realized he didn't recognize her, and the blank first look on his face gave it away. Her self-confidence soared as she was immediately reassured of her look. He was wowed, and she knew it.

Chad was caught off guard and was personally embarrassed. She was only steps from him, and he was unprepared. It was as if the enemy inevitably was approaching, and it was his job to warn the troops of their impending battle. Their survival was dependent upon his early warning. He had failed miserably. He was at a loss for words.

"Wow, you look nice! I like what you did to your hair."

He realized he sounded like a high school kid with a crush. It wasn't just her hair, although he liked the chin length with light blonde highlights. The highlights accented the brunette curls. She tilted her head slightly, and the curls flipped from the side of her face as if she had leaned directly in front of a fan with the speed on high. She wore black leather, form-fitting slacks that tapered inside her gray, calf-length, lace-up, four-inch-high heeled boots. Her long sleeved, white silk blouse was tucked inside her slacks, accenting the silver chain belt that loosely intertwined the loops. The belt looped around past the center of her slacks, dangling down to the middle of her front left pants pocket. The blouse was cause for any man to stare, as well as women. The black buttons of the blouse were unbuttoned mid-chest, gaping open to view her black laced cameo. Her gray shoulder strap handbag was the last touch, which took her forever to find. She wanted it sturdy and durable. She would start at Dillard's on her next shopping spree to save her time and effort.

"I'm glad you like it, but I didn't do anything to it. My hairdresser did."

She smiled at his loss for words. It was comforting to know he noticed her ensemble. It was pricey, but it didn't set her back any either. She could afford it, and she was suddenly aware just how worth the time it was to find the right look.

He grabbed his briefcase, "Do you want to sit here at the bar or go to our seats?"

"I see how it's a business dinner. I'm not sure I'm qualified, but I'll follow you," stepping backwards to allow him to stand from the stool.

He smiled and stood up from the bar, "You want to order a drink before we sit?"

"No, I'm fine, thank you."

As they moved to the rear of the restaurant, she wondered how many glasses of wine he had drunk, or maybe he was just nursing one before she arrived. She couldn't help but notice other guests were dressed to impress. Although he suggested she not go to any lengths with her attire, she was happy with the choices she had made. He was wearing jeans she was sure weren't from a bargain department store. The sport coat he was wearing looked like it was tailored and was accented by his open collar, sky blue, long sleeve shirt. She noticed his gold cufflinks were glimmering, even in the dim lighting. He had warranted a stare from a lady as they approached some open seats. Megan looked at her and then noticed the lady's gaze now focused on her. The lady turned away and glanced down at her plate as if she should apologize to Megan for her inner thoughts. Megan smirked while holding her stare as the lady looked again as they passed.

Empowerment quickly engulfed her. She thought now would be the time to walk tall holding her shoulders back for any others who might wish to stake claim to her date.

He stopped at a booth that had a center table placard with the word "reserved". He gestured with one hand for her to take a seat. She was having second thoughts about buying his dinner. "So, how'd you pull this off? And please don't tell me you know the owner," she said while sliding into her seat.

The reservation was a corner booth near the rear of the restaurant and kitchen. A perfect location to get the waiter's attention at any given moment and privacy from other guests. She was thinking to herself not to blow it and say something immature, turning him off. Her track record with the opposite sex wasn't anything to be proud of. She never saw herself as intimidating, although that is exactly what her female friends had told her many times before. She was feeling particularly out of his league at this very moment.

"I don't know the owner, but I did suggest I would tip well," he smiled, sliding into the seat after placing his satchel on the same seat next to the wall.

"So much for me offering to buy," she smiled, while thinking she was now free to enjoy her dinner.

"Not a chance, this was my idea. You can have the next one."

"There may not be a next one if you see how much I can eat. Besides, if it were left up to me, we'd be looking up at our menu, and they'd be asking if we were wanting to supersize our meal."

"You forget that I've seen you eat. You're smart about it; and besides, there's nothing wrong with splurging occasionally."

"I remember the last time differently. It was from the "Pick-Two" menu, and it was interrupted."

"I never did hear how that ended up. So, what exactly happened?"

Just then a waiter approached and introduced himself. He set glasses of water on the two table coasters and began explaining the evening's dinner special. He was already working his tip, and his mannerism was right on point. Megan declined ordering a drink and explained water was her choice. He asked if they would be interested in an appetizer, and Chad promptly ordered Calamari fries.

"Excellent choice, sir! Can I top off your glass for you?"

"No, thank you-this and the water will be fine," as he was rethinking his decision of having wine.

"Excellent. I'll bring your appetizer right out; take your time," as he removed the coffee cups and saucers from the table and then disappeared to the kitchen.

"You've got to try the fries," in an attempt to soften the idea of her not having a choice of an appetizer. "They're excellent."

"I'm sure they are," while she was still trying to decide if she was comfortable with him ordering anything without her input.

It was a little assertive, but she was not quite sure if it was an attractive trait or not. She was used to being in control. They both were reviewing the menu when Megan decided to break the silence.

"So, what sounds good?"

She already decided on eating light. A dinner salad was something she was looking forward to.

"I'm going with the roasted chicken and steamed broccoli," laying his menu down as he spoke.

Megan continued to look at her choices although she wasn't changing her mind, no matter what he was going to suggest. "Any suggestions?" she asked to see what he would come up with.

"Everything actually looks good, but it's up to you. Whatever you want."

She glanced over the menu smiling at him and then looked back down at her choices. He passed the test she thought to herself.

"I was kind of hoping you would say that," looking over the top of her menu to catch his reaction.

"Absolutely," he responded with a grin.

"Well then, the large tenderloin salad it will be."

"I'm sure it will be good," as he looked directly into her eyes. She noticed how direct his look was. She felt he was looking directly into her soul or perhaps that's just how she wanted him to see her.

"Now, tell me what you heard about Panera," he demanded.

He jumped topics without any hesitation. She knew right away she couldn't guess his actions or what he was thinking. This social setting was much different than helping as her trainer. His focus was much different. He was different. She couldn't grasp who he was at this very moment, all the while realizing he was in fact a total stranger. Although they had been working out in the gym for weeks, she knew absolutely nothing about him. She was glad she drove herself downtown.

"Love triangle gone bad," she pointedly said as she slid her menu to the side. "I couldn't believe no one got hurt. The guy came in and asked to speak to his fiancé's boyfriend. Not that anybody heard what he said, but that's when he shot up the place."

"I bet the boyfriend was glad he didn't take his order," Chad uttered as he shook his head and took a sip of wine.

"It was, apparently, the guy's day off. He wasn't even there."

"My guess is, the wedding was called off," Chad smiled big with the understanding since nobody got hurt, it was easier to joke about it.

"I would suspect," Megan knew he was making light of a serious situation. It was the perfect time to make her move and get all the answers to the questions she wanted or needed from her new-found friend.

"I can't believe you missed the news. It was on several stations," giving him every opportunity to fill her in on his consulting with law enforcement agencies. She knew he was probably in Kentucky helping with all the security surrounding the funeral services.

"I was in Kentucky and out of the loop for any local coverage."

Chad took the bait she was setting for him. Her assumption was confirmed.

"So, you were with all the other cops providing security for people at the Kentucky general's memorial?"

Chad had decided to follow the format, as it was designed to inform a recruit of MoTAF's mission. He wasn't sure if she would believe all of what he was about to tell her or if she even cared. There was a lot to consider especially what she had been through the last year. He was becoming uncertain, uncomfortable, and less confident about the whole idea – his idea.

He reached into his satchel pulling out a manila envelope clasped on the back side. He slid it across the table. "Go ahead; open it. Tell me what you think."

"Your appetizers," said the waiter, setting the plate down between them, and then setting a smaller saucer in front of them both. The waiter opened his notepad and uncapped a pen. "Can I get your orders, or would you prefer a little more time?"

CHAPTER 20

Lex powered-up his computer and monitor. Each keystroke was almost muscle memory, taking him to his usual sites. He hadn't joined in on the conversations but was liking what he was reading. His restraint was because Ruben suggested he not be a participant this soon after being in Kentucky. He wouldn't type anything, not yet. He knew of Ruben's fury and how quickly it rose. Ruben was positive the timing was impeccable to increase the fold and find more who were willing to stand up to the government's strong arm of intimidation.

Lex stared at Ruben who was glued to the mid-day news, "Why do you watch that stuff? It doesn't matter what lies they tell. People can see through it all."

Ruben was not sure what Lex was talking about. He was focused on news segments regarding the Kentucky attorney general's services and all the accolades everyone was saying about him.

"Our Kid got scared or we'd be watching a different kind of news," Ruben snarled. "He got nervous and wanted me to help him with whatever he was planning."

Lex was not sure what he was trying to tell him, but he knew not to ask. He could see his demeanor changing the longer he watched the news. His mind would switch between talking about the Kid, the burner cell he sent him, and what was being said on networks.

"He's been online, but he hasn't mentioned anything about his being at the Kentucky fiasco. I've been reading a lot about it all, and he's kept his head."

"That surprises me, as well," Ruben admitted. "Maybe it's time to do some planning, and this time we'll play in our own backyard."

Lex didn't say a word. He just turned to his monitor and watched what was transpiring. His eyes lit up, and a smile came to his face. He knew Ruben would be pleased to see what he was reading.

"Have you seen this stuff? It's going crazy!" turning to see if Ruben was listening.

Ruben was listening, but he was now focused on his computer screen and not the news feeds. Lex could see he was on split screens keeping tabs on several blogs and social networks. "Our Kid has really stirred things up. He hasn't said anything about being in Kentucky, but he's been watching the news as well and sending his thoughts to anyone who'll listen," Ruben replied.

"Do you think I should reach out to him?" asking in a way that was meant to be a suggestion.

"Absolutely, but keep it simple and bring him in so he will be the one to engage."

Lex knew he couldn't see him roll his eyes. He could almost mouth the words as he spoke. The on-screen language was vile. So much so, Lex couldn't bring himself to be as ruthless. Most participants were right on point, but much of their content got lost in the nonsense. It was almost if a competition was ongoing to see who could outdo the other. Brody was less a participant of over the top dialogue. He was poised and was bringing abundant viewpoints to conversations.

Lex didn't have to wait long before Ruben engaged with the masses. Lex knew it was going to happen. It infuriated him how he was treated as lesser of the duo. He was confident he would find his voice and soon. He wanted a life as well and he realized long ago he had to be smart when it came to Ruben. He couldn't push him over any ledge. His life depended on him being smart.

Ruben started smiling at what was he was seeing. Forums were lighting up with all kinds of conspiracy theories and the like. The corrupt government was doomed, and like minds of Sovereign Patriots were going to bring the country back to where it belonged. If politicians weren't going to do what they were elected to do, consequences would be forced upon them. They were bound to listen to the people, or they would be removed from office.

Ruben was smart enough to understand that those speaking behind each keystroke were the same individuals who wouldn't dare lift a finger to take out their own trash. He found a different mindset in the Kid. He had read enough of the Kid's misfortunes to know he, too, had been thrown to the wolves by those who ran the government systems. The powers that enforced those systems were as much to blame as those who ran them.

When the Kid accepted the cell phone and then used it to contact him, Ruben knew he had a realist, not just an activist. He just needed to school him so that the Kid would work for the Patriots, which would be beneficial to the cause. He had to act smartly.

Ruben was impressed with the Kid. Being in Kentucky, he kept a secret. One could only surmise it was because he didn't want anyone knowing he was there for sinister reasons. He became spooked from all the people who were there and the show of force with the police presence. His identity remained a mystery, even with all the networks he was active in. It was as if he was a ghost and did not exist except through his screen names. That, of course, was how they all were. It was their own safety net.

Ruben found a smart Kid, and he knew it. He picked up on little things, and it was astonishing to see just how much they understood each other. A chat forum was created months ago, and it was the Kid who picked up on the clues to forming a network of devoted, hardened Patriots. The Kid was the only person who picked up on what was said and found himself in company with two other Patriots, Lex and Ruben. It was like an online scavenger hunt. If you get the clue, you can join in the fun. It was in this chat forum where they discussed politics and, more specifically, how corrupt people in power were. They spoke almost code like while in the other chat rooms, discussing why things were the way they were and what should be done about it. It was almost as if there was not anyone else interested in what they were trying to say or just were not smart enough to know what they were saying. Each time the trio found themselves in the secluded forum to chat, no one else joined them. That was fine with Ruben. He didn't like it when there was disagreement, especially when someone was disagreeing with his viewpoint. The forums were always in a room under a different name. If those who were smart enough to grasp the clues to follow, then they were more than welcome to join. When the newcomers became an annoyance, they would find themselves blocked and unable to join the debate. Soon it became apparent, the trio were the only ones conversing. After a fiery exchange regarding elected puppets who were trampling on the Constitution and nearly dismantling the Second Amendment, the Kid threw down a gauntlet, which caught Ruben and Lex both off guard.

"It's time," the words were masterfully spoken. "No longer will devoted Patriots stand idle to what the stars and stripes stand for. We shall never bow to those who relinquish the rights of the majority to serve their own agendas. They shall fall on their own sword."

Brody knew as he typed, that every word was being monitored. He was following script, and he was not about to change course. He didn't quite believe he would be labeled a hero if he assisted in this government takedown, as they called it. After all, it was the government who had ruined his college career with bogus accusations. He still could not believe he was at one moment just a student, and the next, owing thousands of dollars in scholarship money to the university, which just expelled him over nothing. He would play their game as long and as far as they wanted him to. Then, he was getting his life back.

Ruben turned and looked at the back of Lex who was staring at his monitor. "Are you seeing this? He's ready. I think he wants vindication for what he didn't pull off."

"I think you're right. He's ready, but can we trust him?"

"He will know quickly the consequences of betrayal. I assure you of that," Ruben said in his gruff voice. Lex didn't turn around. He knew that tone all too well and what it meant.

Lex and Ruben started interacting in the forum as if they were located halfway across the country from each other. They vowed to support the other and proclaimed extreme allegiance to the Midwestern Patriots.

This geographical announcement gave Brody an opening, "I'm here, as you may well be aware; I just need someone to join me in the fight," he quickly responded to their banter.

Brody, in keeping with his script, was schooled meticulously on how to respond and when to not raise alarm to anyone reading his comments. He was well aware of those who were in the forum and those who were clandestine viewers. He had to be careful but also spot-on with the instructions he was given.

In what seemed almost like Morse Code, Ruben voiced his support to the cause, "You were right to not engage bullies; we will be in our own yard if you want to come play."

The cat and mouse play to get into the private forum was miniscule compared to how open they were chatting now. Any six-year-old could join in on the dialogue and not miss a point. Brody was becoming energized on how well it was all going. He also knew he had to keep his cool. He immediately began to wonder if he was being punked at his expense. Could this all be a set up? Would he soon find himself incarcerated never to be seen again, as promised, if he didn't cooperate? His fingerprints were all over anything that happened from here on out. Whom could he trust, and did he have a choice?

He answered his own questions as he carefully typed, "Let me know when, where, and if I can bring my own toys."

"You'll know when it's time. I'll have something for you to play with. Be ready to travel. It will soon be time," Ruben exited the forum.

CHAPTER 21

"I think we're ready to order," Megan smiled at the waiter and then at Chad. The waiter took both orders and promised to return quickly. He offered Chad another drink as he glanced at his empty wine glass.

Chad declined more wine and opted for coffee, asking the waiter to bring it with his dinner. He hoped his intention for a business meeting was going to be positive. He was certain she had no clue of what kind of consulting he did. He was also confident she would be shocked to learn what he was going to ask of her. He had not quite figured out how he would soften the blow if he could read her reaction well enough. Hopefully, she would be excited to learn more and would agree to become part of something positive.

Chad's mind turned to the intense conversation in the hotel war room. They all conveyed to one another how paramount it was to not let another terrorist attack on democracy occur. For the first time ever, there were rumblings of how something could have been missed from all the clandestine analysts working around the clock. No one went as far as to place blame, but each was determined nothing of similar catastrophic proportions would ever happen in the "Show-Me State".

Analytical conclusions were abundant. They could only surmise that the multiple parties involved were communicating in other ways, either by phone messaging or by meeting in person or at locations known only to them. They had the upper hand and were determined to stop any threat of an attempt to do harm to anyone they had set their sights on.

"So, what do we have here that you may want me to help you with?"

Megan interrupted the zoned-out look he was undoubtedly displaying. She picked up the envelope with the look of uneasiness.

"It's okay, there's nothing in there that will bite."

"I certainly hope not. I'm looking forward to dinner, and I don't want to end up in an E.R. if I can help it."

Cautiously she unclasped the tab and opened the envelope, looking inside as if to make sure nothing was harmful. Her smile was heart-stopping as she looked inside and then up at Chad. He grinned trying to remain focused. He realized everything had just been put in motion, and there was no turning back. This was the first of a long process, and he was hoping he wasn't mistaken in his pursuing her to join in the fight. Due to the urgency of matters at hand, he was sure more than ever she would be a valuable asset.

"Take your time and read it, and then tell me what you think."

Chad knew what she was about to read. He wasn't sure what her reaction would be or, more importantly, why she was being asked to read it.

"*The men and women of MoTAF are dedicated to preserve freedom and democracy within the boundaries of the United States. This mission will not be taken lightly by those who have sworn to uphold it. Those who propose to alter the will of the people will be dealt with extreme prejudice. There will be no afterthought of the welfare of the perpetrator/s. The consequences of their own actions will be the elimination of their existence. The resolve of our state relies in the resiliency of those protecting it.*"

Megan was positive she had read those words before, and she knew exactly where she had seen them. It was the start of her junior year in college. She was looking at the potential legal promise if she could hold steadfast in her academia focus. Her parents repeatedly told her how proud they were of her, and were looking forward to helping her in every way possible toward advancing her legal career. Megan was sitting in her dad's study at their home when he explained why he wanted to study law. He also wanted her to be part of something positive in whatever career path she found herself. It was during that conversation and the reason the father-daughter conversation took place. He wanted to explain to her some of the things he and her mom were entrusted to participate in. They were members of a small group of citizens who were sworn to protect what every moral U.S. citizen holds dear. Megan remembered the words 'MoTAF' as it was emphasized by her dad. He was asking her to consider what it meant and wanted her to find her purpose and maybe work alongside as a family. He was somewhat vague, but he was also resolute in her knowing how private this part of their family was. It was because of that conversation she was unsure what she could reveal to Chad. A new-found friend who just offered her something to ponder and discuss was in stark contrast to the secrecy her father had discussed with her. She was never to speak about the mission of MoTAF outside their home. Why was she reading it again, and why did Chad know about it? She read it again all the while knowing what it said and meant. She was trying to bide her time to come up with the words that would soon be asked of her.

"So, what do you think?"

And there they were. The words came right out, and he was looking at her with an expression of serious reflection.

"What exactly is this?" Megan asked.

"It's something I think you could be part of, an asset for serving a greater cause."

The look on her face proved she was not understanding what was being said.

"I understand what I just read, but don't understand why you had me read it or what you're asking me."

"I know. I was the same way when I read it the first time, too. I didn't understand what was being asked of me. Let me begin by saying, you have people who have watched your collegiate progress."

Megan was listening intently to every word he was saying. She had never met Chad before seeing him at the gym. Since then, they had never talked about where the other was from, although it was kind of understood they were from different backgrounds. How could he know who or why people would know of her degree? She knew he graduated from MIZZOU but was rather surprised she had never met him or even seen him before. He couldn't be more than two years older. With over 30,000 students, she would see the same students everywhere and at multiple times, although she never knew their names. She couldn't understand why she couldn't recall seeing him before. It was starting to overwhelm her.

He explained how he was aware she was finishing her degree online.

He was prepared for all kinds of questions and could tell by the look of amazement on her face there would be several.

"Wait a minute! How do you know I'm finishing my degree online? Why would you know that? We only met a few weeks ago," She started shaking her head and covered her hands over her face.

"Megan, I know some of the same people you know. Like I mentioned before, my undergraduate degree was in psychology. I started my master's program during your sophomore year…"

"Hold on a minute, you know Dr. Morris?"

"Doesn't everybody?" Chad continued all the while noticing her disbelief of them possibly being in the same college circles.

"What's this got to do with MoTAFs' creed?" Megan quickly responded.

She immediately realized what she had said as soon as the words came out of her mouth. It was what her dad called it when they had the discussion about a meaningful purpose in life. A blank look surfaced on Chad's face when she uttered those words.

"What did you say?"

"My dad had a talk with me several years ago. I called it the 'purpose in life' talk. It was about the creed he and mom so much believed in. I was never to mention it to anyone else. I never did. I haven't seen it again until just now."

Chad quickly followed, "What you're saying is you knew what your mom and dad did for the state of Missouri?"

"Not at all. They just wanted me to know there were people who looked out for me and others like me."

Chad paused longer than he intended before speaking. He was not sure how to proceed. He rehearsed the dinner discussion he was planning on having with her. He was now the one with some questions. He wasn't at all sure what he should tell her about MoTAF for fear that she had heard it already.

Megan helped him with his dilemma. "I think I understand now why you brought work with you to dinner," she smiled while picking up the paper and placing it back in the envelope. She took a deep breath to gain back her composure she had lost.

"Can I ask you a question?" she continued not waiting for a reply. "Are you a member of the same thing mom and dad were?"

Chad felt it was time to just wing it and see where things would go. "Yes, I worked with your mom and dad." He looked at her trying to decipher her thoughts.

"I never thought I'd be sitting with a mere stranger talking about my parents." She took a sip of water to sooth the lump in her throat and forced back the emotions. She started telling herself, now is not the time. She refused to let herself cry in front of him.

"I would say I know how you feel, but I don't." Chad thought now would be the time to tell her more about himself, but he wasn't sure about the timing. "I never knew my parents; I never had a place I could actually call my home."

Chad began the short version of his life story. The abbreviated version was not what he had planned for dinner conversation. He could only hope that she would be willing to listen to the full version later. There was an upside to his abbreviated version. She did not get up and leave. She sat there and listened about his adolescent years. He put a spin on it, so it was not depressing for her to hear all of what he was saying. She could easily find herself in overload mode. He was determined to avoid that type of emotional drama, but she had to hear about some of his rough times. He was putting elements of his degree to work. He had to be sure she was emotionally available to tackle the challenging events MoTAF was currently experiencing. She seemed to listen, listen well, and he was appreciative of that fact.

The timing for the waiter bringing their entrées was perfect. It caused a lull in what had become a rather solemn conversation. She finally spoke and brought back the mood of which she apparently wanted to remain solemn.

"How were you able to get out of the situation you were in growing up?"

"I didn't do anything. My foster parents homeschooled me and found out I was gifted. They believed in me, and I channeled that energy for MU scholarships." This was the window of opportunity he had been waiting for.

"Megan, there are people all over the country who want to harm others. We have our share right here in Missouri. It's serious, and it's happening now." He could tell she was listening to his every word.

"What do you mean it's happening? What's happening?"

"It's complicated. It's serious, and it's something I'm reluctant to fully disclose right now," he replied, as he looked down at his clasped hands that encircled the coffee mug the waiter had just filled for him.

He was charting in unfamiliar waters and wasn't confident with discussing his clandestine work. He knew the dinner would be difficult because of his introducing her to what he did. He did not, however, like the feeling of being so inept. He had rehearsed what he was going to say to her and how he would answer the questions she would undoubtedly ask.

She had a smirk on her face, and it slowly turned into a huge smile. It caught him off guard. He couldn't believe what was happening. He was being serious, and she was laughing at him.

"What's so funny?" he asked her in a low monotone voice to minimize his disappointment of her amusement. "How is domestic terrorism funny?"

"It's not. What's funny is what you've been trying to say to me. It's obvious you're wanting to ask me something."

He had been so coy in what he thought was going to be difficult for her to understand. He had come to the realization it was he who was having a problem.

"I'd ask you to come right out and say what you've been wanting to, but I think I already know what it is."

She leaned forward with both palms on the table. She was enjoying her dinner, and what was becoming rather humorous was that Chad was charmingly uncomfortable. He was attempting to be cautious in what he was trying to say, and he was failing miserably.

"You do, do you? I'm not at all sure what it is I'm trying to say. What do you know about the creed?" Chad asked.

"My dad had me read that years ago." She picked up the envelope as to reference its contents. "He told me about some things he and mom were involved with, which were fulfilling and rewarding."

Chad couldn't believe what was happening. She was aware of what he did; and, more importantly, what her parents did. There was nothing he could have done to prepare for what was happening to his rehearsed dinner conversation.

"Chad, I'm not at all sure what you do, but I know now what kind of consulting work you're involved in."

The evening could not have been more confusing for Chad. He was not in control. He was accustomed to being the lead consultant of all that involved MoTAF. He knew he was not in control or perhaps he never was. She was very capable of being a player and not being played. Because of being unsure of what was going to happen next, he was beginning to lose his appetite.

Megan monopolized the conversation from that point on. She began to inform what little she knew about MoTAF. What started out as an interesting dinner turned into a teachable moment for Chad. He was unaware of most of what she was telling him. The episodes involving MoTAF were enlightening and intriguing. He had heard of some of the events from other analysts, but what Megan was telling him occurred before he was recruited. Her father was very thorough but at the same time kept much of the behind-the-scenes information from her. She never learned what happened to those who meant to do harm, other than they were dealt with.

"Let me make myself perfectly clear," Megan continued. "I'm all into becoming a force that is meaningful and fulfilling. I want to be part of something special. Something I know my parents would be proud of. I wasn't sure who was working with them. Now I know you were. I want to join you in the fight."

CHAPTER 22

Lex had to make his reluctant phone call. He was asked, or rather told, by Ruben to make sure he had everything he needed before he left for Jefferson City. He was to leave by eight in the morning, looking the part. He was to dress in business attire and blend in with any pre-event planning that was occurring at the state Capitol and keep him apprised of everything.

Lex had only been in Jefferson City long enough to make one circle around the state Capitol. He finally was able to park on the circle drive and make the call.

Just as suspected, Ruben was less than pleased when he got his awaited call.

"I've been waiting for your call. You were supposed to call me as soon as you got there."

Lex had almost forgotten about the friend locator app they both had on their phones. Ruben would turn his app off frequently. Lex was once threatened when the app wasn't working on his phone. Ruben had gone into another one of his rants Lex was sure to remember. He again accused Lex of uninstalling the app on his phone and then reinstalling it, which would cause the interruption in the app.

Lex tried to explain. "I haven't had a chance to look at …"

"The Kid is going to need a high vantage point and so will I." Ruben's interruption was infuriating. "Find one both on the inside and out and get back to me."

Ruben had not given Lex an exact plan of events or what his thoughts were on what was going to take place. It was not the first time he had kept him in the dark. It was like he was supposed to know without being told. It was frustrating, and Lex was determined to settle the score in that department. He did not know when or how but was sure it was going to happen. Ruben had concluded the call as he did many times before. He would stop talking, the connection would end, and there would be silence.

Lex had his orders and knew what needed to be done. He was not sure what exactly would take place, but he was sure it was going to be huge. There were a lot of Patriots wanting to be part of something exciting. These were the same who wouldn't get off the couch to get their own can of beer, if it was not for someone telling them how to go about doing it. Lex was smitten by Ruben in the fact that he was intelligent. Smart to a fault, but nonetheless he was very analytical with how things should be done. He often thought if Ruben were a CEO of a Fortune 500 company, it would thrive. Instead, they both were working for a lawn company.

Lex observed signs of limited parking. He had two hours to look over the interior of the Capitol. He had scoped out places before. He would not leave any stone unturned. There had to be contingencies for every scenario. He checked the battery on his cell, and it was almost fully charged. He would take as many pictures and videos as he could without causing suspicion. He would trace steps and mark distances for what may be needed. He would act like a tourist and look the part, as well. Ruben had told him to dress in business attire, but he knew he had to look like a tourist. What tourist would be in a sport coat or tie?

He located the handicap parking and what entrances were accessible from those parking areas. He walked the entire exterior of the Capitol noticing multiple entrances and exits.

What was most noticeable were the security cameras mounted at each entrance, as well as every exterior vantage point imaginable. To Lex it was a little unnerving, knowing he was being watched at every turn. It was also understandable. Although he hadn't been in very many statehouses around the country, Missouri's was the one place that was easily accessible for any wrong doers. Although there were uniformed security officers who walked each of the five granite floors, there were no magnetometers. Anyone could carry a bazooka through any doorway. No alarms would sound, although people would get on their cells and the police foot patrol would attempt to rectify the problem. By then, of course, it would be too late. If hearing rooms were packed with people, they would all perish following one slight pull of a trigger. The cameras were perhaps going to be a problem. They seemed to be at every turn, and the recordings were housed in a location known to only those who were viewing them.

Lex made several trips to each floor. He found the elevator as well as the stairwells. Two stairwells were not marked but located on the east and west end of the Capitol. It was by accident he found them. While walking down what seemed to be one of the hidden stairwells, he found the basement parking garage. It was obvious the interior parking was for the elite. State license plates were on most of the double-parked cars. Each parking stall had numbers, which did not seem to correlate with the state license plate attached to the car that was parked. The cars were stacked close and doubled in each location. There were signs reminding those parking to leave keys with their vehicles for easy movements to allow those blocked in to be able to leave the parking garage.

Lex's watch chimed. The alarm he set on his phone gave him ample time for him to return to his car for the two-hour parking restriction. He walked toward an unfamiliar door leading to a hallway. He saw several people walk through the door and he wanted to see where it led. As he walked through the door, he saw the words: "Private Parking – Chief Executive." In that reserved parking spot was a black, GMC Yukon Denali SUV. It had several antennae on the roof. Lex could see blue and red lights strategically mounted to the interior of the front windshield. An unexpected find and a perfect one at that.

Lex followed what appeared to be young employees walking to offices. They all knew where they were going because they entered unmarked doorways without announcing themselves. There was an exit sign that led to the outside. He got his bearings after exiting the Capitol and found his car. There was no ticket on the windshield after returning in ample time. He couldn't afford a ticket with license and vehicle information entered in any police database. He needed to make more steps and acclimate himself to the Capitol interior. He found a gift he didn't expect to find. The governor's reserved parking and his mode of transportation. Ruben would be pleased.

"That's outstanding!" Ruben uttered into his phone. "This is better than expected."

This was a first for Lex. He had never heard that much excitement in Ruben's voice. He had reported back from something he was ordered to do and had succeeded in pleasing the devil.

"I've only been able to find the entrances, stairwells, and elevators. I had to return to my car and move it to avoid any parking tickets."

"You've got a couple more days. That should be ample time to scope out everything. We now have a 'plan C' we can work on. I'll let you know what I come up with."

"What about our senator? Do you still want me to visit him and get VIP credentials?"

"This event isn't going to require any specific credentials to get up close. I've rethought the issue. If we find ourselves as volunteers, we'll end up answering phones in a small room without any windows. No, we've got to be able to be mobile and pull this off like all our other stealth Patriot missions."

"I'll see what I can find out and get back with you," Lex said, as Ruben once again abruptly ended the call.

Brody got a "ping" on his new cell phone. It was the one phone he hated. It was not an alert he chose, and he did not like the feature. The apps on the phone were worthless; they didn't work. It had only one purpose, and that was what the government wanted. It was the right price. It was given to him as a gift, a gift he preferred not to receive. A gift from the federal government which was, once again, ruining his life. He had concluded he was in a "no-win" situation. He was smart enough to know he couldn't outsmart them. He unwillingly had to decide to play their game. It was a game that he did not like being part of. He understood he made the wrong decision with some unsavory characters. He wanted a normal life again and hoped he'd get back what was left of it. He was staying out of jail, and he would do anything to not be in any interrogation room again with guys who could make him disappear forever.

All the while Brody was certain his life would never be the same, he was also intrigued. He had witnessed things he had only seen in movies and turned him even more against any authoritative figure. How could the government own anybody? It was not fair. However, he was impressed with how they knew who he was and everything important about him. The mere fact that he wasn't in jail, being charged with any crime, or going on trial for something he knew he was guilty of, fascinated him. He was caught attempting to commit the most heinous of crimes, and now he was unwillingly assisting someone, that he was sure was getting ready to do the same. These were the very same people who led him down a treacherous path, a path he was now sure was not the right one. It was cleverly explained; his own actions would have soon caused his own death. He was convinced the people he deplored had saved his life. He would have a future. It was up to him what he would make of it. A strange turn of events turned his life around in a fashion no one would believe. But, then again, who could he tell? There was not anyone he was close enough to that he could tell. Brody was beginning to think his life was already over and there was no happy ending to what he was currently experiencing.

People he had not met would have eventually killed him. It was obvious why these saviors wanted the big fish in the pond. He was not so sure the people who saved him were going to be able to catch who they were looking for. That put him in the cross hairs, and he was sure that was not where he wanted to be. How was it that he turned so easily? Now he was assisting in the hunt for the same people he had become? It almost seemed like a dream, but he was sure it was not. There was no need to think he was going to wake up to anything different than the reality he was currently in.

The "ping" on his phone was his cue. He knew his new-found friends wanted him to lure the enemy. The enemy was online. It was time for him to find out what it was he needed to do for the Patriots--his Patriots. It was becoming all too weird. He was being lured in to kill--something he was not sure he was ready to do. He now had to make sure his Patriot friends were blind to the fact he was not their friend. They were to assume he had the backbone to kill for the cause--a cause he now did not recognize. He was pretty sure he knew who he could trust, although it wasn't as if he had any choice in the matter. Not much of it made any sense to him anymore. He had to do what he was told. It was the only way he was certain he could salvage what he treasured, his freedom. He also was not certain what that was anymore. Although he was free from incarceration, he knew he was a long way from being a free man.

He wasn't surprised at what he found when signing into his favorite social media sites. The forum was lit up with all kinds of vulgarity. The posts were getting rather boring. He was not all that crazy about reading it before and didn't join in with the same vulgar commentary. Now, it was becoming annoying. Although he tolerated it before, it now sickened him. Had he changed that much in such a short time?

He got his cue to enter the adjacent online forum. He knew who it was but wasn't sure how many would be there when he changed screen portals. What he did know was that he would be watched. Not just him, but everyone in the forum would be watched by the agency he now was siding with. Every keystroke would be used for or against them depending on which side of patriotism they would choose.

CHAPTER 23

The video conference had ended. It was another first. Although Chad was involved in the one following the 9-11 attacks, he was also intimately involved with all facets of Missouri's frontline defense. The conference call from analysts outlined what was revealed from the online conversations. They were together by video conference the same week the towers fell. Following that initial gathering, a successful recruitment drive took place. The state was separated by zones with the largest encompassing the cities of St. Louis, Kansas City and, the third-largest city in the state, Springfield. Not since then had there been this large a number of domestic conspirators who were actively engaging and threatening the state's core fabric of democracy. At least none they were aware of. Without a strong government, democracy would cease to exist. A fragmented government from violence would eventually lead to tyranny. There was already enough violence and civil unrest across the country. The crumbling of democracy in the heart of America would spread like a plague. If that happened, the states would no longer be united.

Someone lit the wick to the powder keg, and it was going to explode. The Sovereign Patriots were planning something in Jefferson City. The exact place and time were the unknown variables that needed to be solved. Discussion was weighed on the chance of communicating to the Patriots in hopes of talking them down. That was the easy way out. They all knew it was futile attempting diplomatic solutions to radical mindsets. They had already shown no mercy for their cause. The consensus was unanimous. No mercy would be shown for those who vowed to bring terrorist activity to the "Show-Me State".

Chad had planned and prepared for whatever was to happen. He was going in the field, and what better time to bring Megan into the effort. It was imperative they succeed; there was not a choice. What occurred in Kentucky could happen in Missouri if something was not done to prevent it. Megan had to be brought in and briefed on everything. She was so receptive to being part of MoTAF, but would she be as excited when she realized the danger?

Chad had driven to the gym and waited in the parking lot. A text was sent to Megan earlier after the conference call. He made sure she had a few hours to spare and to meet him at the gym. She was curious and intrigued when he mentioned it wasn't going to be a workout session. He was wanting to talk business about MoTAF and had an offer he wanted her to consider.

He had to brief her on what had transpired and bring her up to speed. If she had been keeping up with any current events, some of what he was going to tell her would make some sense. Otherwise, she would probably have more questions than he would have answers. But, of course, that was what he had expected before. Recruitment rules had obviously changed. If she had specific inquiries, he hoped Brian could answer them. She knew of him and trusted him with her money. Hopefully she would not be too shocked to learn he was part of MoTAF, as well. She was now one of many who were sworn to protect what they all cared about, the place where they lived, their family, and their friends.

It was a short drive to his home. She did more listening during the ride than inquiring about where they were going. She knew it was important, and the seriousness of the drive became clear when they passed through the gated entrance.

Chad led Megan into the basement of his home. She did not speak; she just followed. She stopped at the bottom of the staircase looking at the monitors and computer screens. Most of the screens were dark with no one sitting in the high back chairs in front of them. She took in how spacious and comfortable the surroundings seemed. A conference table had a dozen chairs around it with a large flat screen centered on a wall at one end. Megan was impressed, recognizing what seemed like a high-tech military war room but could pass for a conference room of a multi-million-dollar business. She could hear, just above muted volume, voices of multiple national news programs on different televisions programming simultaneously discussing their priority topics of the day.

"Join us; make yourself at home," said Chad, who had not stopped at the bottom of the steps.

It was at that moment when one of the high-back leather chairs spun around. Brian smiled at Megan as their eyes met.

"Welcome, Megan. Can we get you something to drink?"

"Hi, Brian."

She tried to not look surprised, but it was obviously too late. Her financial advisor was obviously Chad's as well.

"I would say funny to see you here but it's rather obvious, I'm the one who's the guest." Her smile was once again mesmerizing.

Chad was beginning to understand her smile was also one of her defense mechanisms. She was apprehensive, and Chad was recognizing the hints.

"Please, feel at ease. Let me get you something to drink, or you can help yourself. A kitchenette is right over there, and the fridge is stocked." Chad gestured to the area just off from the conference table.

Megan had not noticed the small kitchen area. "Thank you, but I'm fine." Her smile continued as she tried to hide what was becoming an even more awkward moment.

Chad uttered in a business mannerism, "Like I told you on the drive over, we're involved in an ongoing clandestine operation. We want you to understand the stakes and let you decide how involved, if at all, you want to become."

Brian noticed the way she looked at him. It was as if, she was in a dream and was not sure how it was going to end. He motioned to a chair in front of a coffee table, and they all sat down at once.

"Megan, let me start by saying I'm here to help ensure things go smoothly with the operation." Brian tried to assure what he hoped was the obvious. "You're probably wondering what exactly is my function."

Brian began explaining how he became involved with MoTAF, starting with his background as a CPA. Although he was a financial advisor and consultant for several clients including Megan, he was the money-man behind all MoTAF's functions. He explained how funding through the Department of Homeland Security kept MoTAF running smoothly. There was nothing they couldn't acquire due to the unlimited federal funding source. He tried to explain things rather simply, so she wouldn't ask many questions, although he assumed she would. He paused several times and asked if she was following what he was telling her. This, too, was new to Brian. He had not had to explain his function in MoTAF before under such extraordinary circumstances.

"Things are moving at a very rapid pace," Chad said. "We need to get you up to speed as quickly as possible."

Chad had thoroughly explained MoTAF's operations and reiterated their sworn mission. It was apparent that Megan was taken aback by all the computer monitors, the conference room itself, and the other accommodations. She was quickly understanding Chad's home was not just any regular bachelor's pad. It was a very formal and business atmosphere, although no one dressed the part.

"It's my understanding Chad has filled you in on what he does. I want to let you in on what's taking place here in our state and what we are doing to stop the serious threats facing us."

Megan calmed her nerves and said, "I have to admit I'm a little surprised by his skill set."

Brian began by explaining how some of the current newsworthy events were not what they seemed. He continued to enlighten her on how a college student became involved and how his relentless coercions and planning had now become part of the Department of Defense's line of defense.

"But why isn't this guy in jail?" Megan asked.

"Simply put," Chad answered, "he hasn't been caught by law enforcement. MoTAF is not a police force. We are, like I explained, a clandestine organization."

When Brian began explaining the chain of events in Kentucky, he and Chad could see the shock and surprise on her face. It was like she was watching a movie unfold in front of her. They also noticed the change in her demeanor as they explained how they could view the potential planning of an upcoming attack. Chad explained they were in the early stages of preventing an attack. All that was needed was a more precise threat and who it was they were looking for. Megan then asked the question they had hoped she would.

"What can I do to help?"

With a most stern, narrow-eyed stare, Brian answered, "We want you to understand the danger involved. This is nothing like you've ever been close to before regarding potential loss of life--yours."

"I understand. Yes, but it's the same for you guys as well."

Chad and Brian explained how every precaution would be taken. It was their hope, as well as everyone's, that the terrorists would see how unwise it was to go through with their plan or any other. Realistically, they realized from what had already occurred, there was a good chance that whatever they were planning was going to come to an unfortunate end for someone.

"What kind of weaponry are you guys equipped with?" Megan continued. "I'm only familiar with GLOCK."

Chad looked over at Brian with a smile, and Brian returned one of the same. They were surprised by her frank questions and, especially, how they planned to protect themselves.

"I think we'll be just fine. Keep in mind we have the federal government at our disposal," Brian answered.

Chad asked, "Megan, did you bring your GLOCK as I suggested? We want to expose you to some shoot, don't shoot scenarios. We have erected advanced training targets at a range behind the house."

"I brought my GLOCK. I hardly go anywhere without it anymore. I only have one mag with me, though." Chad and Brian opened a locker showing Megan some of their tools of the trade.

"They are fun to shoot," Brian said, as he pulled out an AR-15 and handed it to Megan. "Ammo can be hard to find for some people. We're OK in that department as well."

Megan was impressed with the range located in Chad's backyard. Assailant life-size targets, as well as hostage targets, were set up at various distances. They all took turns engaging multiple targets, while moving through the shooting range distances. Megan was always the last of the three to go through each scenario. Megan impressed her trainers while using the weapon her dad trained her on. Chad and Brian had no concerns with her shooting ability and would inform all associates how Megan managed the indoctrination. They hid their amazement on how well she grasped everything given to her. Their accelerated plan was working.

CHAPTER 24

Lex was amazed how he wouldn't even get a second glance from anyone about his fake driver's license and the fact he never used a credit card for any of his purchases. He was never questioned on the license plate he would write down when at hotels. He always made up one when checking into a hotel. People were just too trusting. His smile, so he thought, was probably what brought him such good luck, and, of course, his award-winning personality. Little did they know, he was a Patriot ready to make a name for himself and other Patriots like him.

It was time for an update. He knew he didn't want Ruben to call him. He would say he would call but would be thoroughly disappointed and want to know why he had not heard how things had been going. Another downside to calling was getting his voicemail recording. You could never leave a message because his phone had never been set up for receiving messages. He always wanted to hear what anybody wanted to say to him in real time. It was frustrating knowing he wanted to know what was going on but didn't want to be bothered by multiple calls if he wasn't ready to talk.

Ruben picked up on the second ring. He was not wanting any pleasantries when talking on the phone. "What do you have for me? Any surprises you weren't expecting?"

"The only surprise was the Capitol. There were little to no precautionary measures for security. There were armed officers roaming the halls, but it seems to be a limited number at any given time. I didn't see more than the same five or six, whichever floor I walked. They didn't pay any attention to me, but I didn't want them to see me more than twice. I think I fit in just fine."

"What about exterior elevated positions?"

"That is where a problem may become an issue. The surrounding state buildings didn't have easy rooftop access. All access doors, which were on the top floors, were secured with proximity keypads or regular turnkey locks for access. There are no exterior stairs that lead to the upper floors."

"What you're saying is we are basically out of luck with finding a high vantage point."

"That's correct. There are no parking garages in this town anywhere close to the Capitol."

Lex was bracing himself for what he was sure to be name-calling and cursing, but it never came.

"Two days, that's all the time we've got. I'll have this nailed down to an artful masterpiece. I'm going to get our Patriot Kid to join us. This Friday is going to be memorable for the 'Show-Me State'."

Ruben got online to see if his friends were there and to see if anyone had any knowledge of anything noteworthy. He quickly became frustrated with the nonsense he was reading. He became incensed with how naïve they all seemed. They fed off each other and were rather childish in their uneducated political rhetoric. Some seemed well versed, but most were far from having intellect to carry on simple grade school historical conversations. He continuously found himself trying to educate and inform them on political correctness but was dumbfounded, realizing very few could grasp what he was trying to tell them. "Millennials" are what they call themselves, but Ruben had a different name for them, which he felt was much more appropriate.

Brody got an alert on his phone. He hated the alert because he knew who it was from and why he was receiving it. The analysts were monitoring specific websites, blogs, and social media where freedom Patriots were frequenting. He was being summoned to join in on social media where he was to converse and entice. He was not at all comfortable with it but realized he had not been given a choice. This, in and of itself, infuriated him. He felt like he had to stay in his one-bedroom apartment just waiting for the fed phone to sound off.

There was a fine line between entrapment and doing what he was told to do. As far as he was concerned, there wasn't any difference, and any two-bit attorney could prove it. He only hoped it would not come to that. The way things were going thus far, he would become a statistic.

He logged in as usual. There was one screen name monopolizing the blog as usual. He presented himself informed and intelligent. Although he never would say what his IQ was, he would jokingly say smart people never let on just how dumb they are.

Brody was drawn to the dialogue and mesmerized once again. He did not even join in the fun when he noticed he was leaving the blogosphere to the all-familiar site. Brody knew what that meant when Ruben left the one forum. Although Brody never knew his real name, he knew where he could privately chat with him. The very first comment to him was shocking. Butterflies of fear went rushing through Brody's gut. It was like everyone was in the flesh, standing right next to him in the room-- all of them waiting for a response to the question.

"I'm assuming you got my packages?"

He was not sure how to respond. He could hardly ask what it was, although he knew he should. He had not received anything, and he also knew the ghost visitors were also waiting. He had to follow the script, although there was not one. He had to play it smart.

"Just like before, it isn't my birthday, and it sure isn't Christmas," he responded.

"These little gifts cost me more than expected. You may have to start bringing your own toys," Ruben quipped.

"I have. Don't you recall?"

Brody was grasping at straws. He had no idea what he was being asked. He was at a loss as to how he should respond to something he didn't understand.

"I'm assuming you haven't gotten them yet. I can track to see where they are, but..."

"I'll sign for them once the packages arrive." Brody felt reprieved.

"It will be one package with two toys. I hope your bags are packed. You have two days to get to our capital city. Instructions are included."

Analysts had arranged for a conference call following their clandestine visit with the terrorists. Chad joined the analysts' conference call. They were all surprised a time frame had been determined. The unidentified subject was planning a terror attack, but the what, when, and where was not quite clear. They had gotten a big break and were going to capitalize on it at their first opportunity. The Capitol would be the obvious location, but who would be targeted? The analysts discussed a possible catastrophic attack on the building resembling the Oklahoma City bombing. The discussion was quickly dismissed because most concurred the intelligence revealed a small, not large, group to pull off an attack of such magnitude. Chad argued to no avail about the number of suspects it took to pull off the attack in Oklahoma. The frustration was at a boiling point when Megan tapped his right arm gently. The gentle smile she gave him soothed his temperament. It was a place he had not found himself in recent memory. He was appreciative of Megan's calming presence at a time he needed it most.

It was obvious everything was Kentucky-related. The search for a probable Missouri target would have political ramifications. There was little chance to alert a possible target as well as identify the assailants. The assailants had to be stopped. The clock was ticking, and all resources were needed to prevent the unthinkable. The issue at hand was no one knew what the assailants looked like or who they were. Nor did anyone know whose life was being threatened.

Analysts were traveling to help neutralize the threat, whomever it may be. Publicizing MoTAF was not something that was discussed, and preventing a terrorism event without involving federal, state, and local authorities wasn't going to be an easy feat.

Anonymous credible contact with local law enforcement had been successfully conducted in other states. Missouri was a prime candidate for pulling out all the stops. It had to be done. An imminent attack was going to occur.

CHAPTER 25

Ruben, Lex, and the Kid had been talking using the multi-voice data service package purchased on the new cell phones they all had. They had gone dark with the on-line planning, and all converged in the capital city. They found no trouble with their fake identifications they used to make their lodging arrangements. They all stayed at different, modest locations throughout town. Their lodging had long been secured by a business account under one of the many false names Ruben had obtained over the years. Cash was drawn from ATM's in locations a minimum of thirty miles from the county of where they were intending to lodge. Masks or disguises were used at the ATM's for precautionary reasons so as to not identify the users if video security programs were used. Ruben was appreciative of paperless banking institutions. It served his purpose very well.

Lex and the Kid followed their instructions to the letter. They were afraid of the consequences of doing otherwise. They all used the drive-through, fast-food restaurants, Ruben choosing the only Chick-fil-A in town. He then pulled into the farthest parking of the Lowe's Home Improvement Center normally used by their employees. No video surveillance cameras were visible and there were none on the market that could identify their vehicles or anything about them at those distances. Lex and Brody pulled into the same parking lot a short distance from each other at nearly the same time. Ruben pulled up to Lex and waved for him to get in. Lex got in the front seat, and Ruben drove a short distance further to Brody. He was signaled as well, and Brody immediately got into the rear seat.

Ruben glanced into his rearview mirror. "Hello, Kid. I'm Ruben. Say 'hello' to Lex."

Lex turned and shook Brody's hand as Ruben pulled away. They had no clue where they were going, but neither of them spoke. The state Capitol dome could be seen from miles away. It was apparent they were probably heading to the state's governmental centerpiece.

Ruben circled the Capitol, and then one block later noticed the security cameras perched at the Governor's Mansion boundary. The historic masterpiece sat in the heart of the downtown district backing up to the mighty Missouri River. He could not be sure about the security around Missouri's chief executive's residence. It remained a secret. No research was available on the topic, although it was probably certain a low bid was the norm for state contracting services. Motion sensor technology was likely in the sod and within the floral and hedge landscaping. With the high vantage buildings and the natural tall trees surrounding the adjacent governor's garden, a breach of the plush grounds would be risky and probably unsuccessful. It would be time consuming formulating a plan to break onto the mansion grounds and into the mansion itself. The armed security force at the governor's residence maintained a two-to-the-chest, one-to-the-head, no-nonsense reputation.

The residence was historic as well as majestic. A lesson was easily learned from a simple call to the phone number on the Governor's Mansion Tours web site. A request for a collegiate tour for a history class found the weakest link was not in the security or its technology, but in policy. The receptionist, who answered questions, unknowingly admitted the mansion was a soft target. Although not publicized, it's well known, the security force at the Missouri Governor's Mansion are manned by commissioned officers. They just preferred to disallow other forms of weapons on the premises. The softer target would be the office where the governor conducted his business. When the time came, and a Sovereign Patriot lived in the mansion, a need to breach the security would not be necessary. Invitations to come and dine would be the norm.

The flagpole positioned in the nearest corner to the city's downtown district seemed to symbolize stability. The raised colors of the prisoner-of-war, state, and U.S flags, flew flawlessly as busy people made their way to wherever they had to be. No one seemed to even glance toward the mansion or the flags as they nearly unfolded completely in the breeze. The mansion had become just another building among all the others. The occasional photo spot was an obvious telltale sign of those visiting the capital city. Ruben was not going to be one of those obvious visitors. He wanted his trio to blend in with those around him; he did not want to unduly stand out. They were just people in the crowd, in a busy city, doing what busy people do-or not do. They would look long and hard, to no avail, for him or his friends. He had created another perfect plan to remove the chief executive. He had become one of the reasons Patriots were rising across the country and taking arms to take back what was sacred: freedom.

As Ruben slowed for the intersecting traffic light at the mansion, he uttered to his passengers, "Those flags will fly half-mast after tomorrow."

The stealth plan was in place just like before. This time, however, Ruben's target was unmistakable, and the execution would be carried out with marked precision. The mission would gain Patriot notoriety and the desired national attention.

He continued driving east on Capitol Avenue, then turned south, pulling to a textbook stop at a stop sign. Security cameras were mounted on the Sheriff's Department building across from them. He wondered if the low bid security cameras would even detect license plates from where they were positioned. By the angle and position of the cameras, it appeared the department's main concern was who is approaching and entering the front doors from their parking lot. There were no exterior cameras at the library across the street, and the courthouse security measures were undoubtedly on the interior. Ruben pulled into the first available parking spot and shut the engine off.

"This is where it all begins. Everything will center around the responses to downtown. There could be a change in the plan, so be ready."

The plan was meticulous. Lex expected nothing less. Brody felt he was out of their league and just sat patiently, not knowing whether to speak. Ruben repeatedly asked each one his task and when it was to occur. They sat in discussion until everything was perfect in the planning. It was repeated several times; both Lex and Brody knew not to make a mistake in the outline of events.

"We're ready, guys. Sovereign Patriots across the country will be proud."

Another set of burner phones was handed out. Like before, they would be immediately discarded once their one-time use was completed. Brody felt nauseous. He fought back the feeling of revisiting his lunch. If Ruben or Lex found out he was being watched and was a snitch for the feds, he knew his life would be in danger. It was in danger as it was. The ride back to their cars was another trip, and words were not spoken. Brody was sure the parking lot would be surrounded by police waiting for their return, but everything was normal. He knew he was becoming paranoid. He had to somehow get out of his predicament and resume a normal life. There was plenty of time to think about the path his life had taken and what steps he needed to take for righting the ship. Could he trust the feds? Deep within his inner soul, he felt they could not be trusted this time either, but what choice did he have?

Brody walked into the hotel lobby with a nervous feeling. Everyone who glanced at him made him uneasy. He felt like he could not trust anyone. The fact of the matter was, he couldn't. He went into his room and sensed it had been entered. What he had already gone through was becoming too much. His paranoia was getting the best of him. He reached into the bottom of his satchel of clothes and pulled out his fed phone. Three missed calls and one text message. There was no indication of a voice message waiting to be heard, just the number of calls and the one text.

"Make yourself available. We are needing an update."

He drafted a reply text message. It took him longer than expected. He wanted to tell them where he was and what he had been doing, but he could not be certain who would be receiving it. Would they use it against him to warrant the death penalty? He found himself in a non-trusting environment and was not sure how to get out of it. He had to follow the plan, which had been laid out. He knew if he did what the Patriots were planning, his life would end being incarcerated. If he failed the Patriots, his life would undoubtedly end prematurely. He had to trust somebody; he felt alone. He needed to be able to sleep. He was smart enough to realize his mental health was in jeopardy.

"I couldn't have the phone with me. We were planning tomorrow's events. I want out." He pressed "send" and flopped down on the bed.

He needed to figure a way out of this madness. Things had gone too far. His phone made an annoying sound. Afraid to look at the message, he thought about pressing delete without reading it. He knew there was no way out. He had to let happen whatever was going to happen. He had no other choice.

His phone chirped again. "You'll be free of all things tomorrow. We'll help you get out. Just follow our instructions. Answer your room phone… now." The ring startled him. Although he was reading that he was going to receive a call, he still wasn't expecting it. Did they know where he was? His paranoia was starting to take over. He wasn't sure he should answer the phone or talk to anyone.

"Hello, who is this?"

"Listen Brody, we are here to help you. Remember, if we wanted, you'd be locked away somewhere for a very long time."

"I can't do this anymore. They are going to kill the governor. I don't want any part of this anymore."

"We put a tracker on your car and your friend's car at Lowe's earlier today in case we lost you during our surveillance. There's a lot of stuff we can do Kid. With the phone we gave you, we can trace your location and merge it through analog and digital convergence to the burner phone you have. You'll not read any of that in a tech magazine."

"They gave me another phone."

"Brody, we know already. We got this. You have nothing to worry about."

He was told they got some good pictures of him and the suspected Patriots. While they were parked downtown, some of those passing by were members of MoTAF. Others were people he had met before during some of his memorable encounters on his college campus. The Patriots were followed from there by unsuspecting motorists. They had to believe they were not being followed. It was obvious they were being cautious. They both made several trips to other parts of the city and even across the river and back before going to their respective hotels. Brody drove straight from Lowe's to his hotel.

Brody explained they were in disguise, so the pictures may not be of any use. He was told they also had their license plates, which surprisingly weren't stolen. From the registered vehicles, the Department of Revenue provided color photos. Brody listened to the friendly voice on the phone.

He was obviously shaken and didn't think he could go through with it. He was losing it. The voice was calming perhaps because it was a female.

"I can leave now and go to a place where they'll never find me," Brody nervously stated. "I think I'm being set up. Everyone could be going to pin this on me, including you guys."

The calm voice on the other end continued in her reassuring tone. "Go down to the lobby, and grab a cup of complimentary coffee. A guy will ask you if you want to read the USA Today newspaper that he just finished looking at. Tell him what you know about tomorrow then take the newspaper to your room. Ruben or Lex did not follow you. You're safe. Pay close attention to the sports page."

The phone line went dead. He sat up in bed and quickly made a path to the bathroom. He heaved into the toilet until his abdomen ached. He splashed cold water on his face to compose himself and then left to go to the lobby. On the elevator from the third floor, Brody remembered being told they were aware of their identity. He wasn't just being paranoid. He was being watched. They knew their names and what they looked like. They even knew what room he was in. He rationalized their blown identity was a good thing. He was beginning to think, perhaps he could walk away from it all.

Megan wasn't accustomed to lying. She didn't answer his question as to what her name was. She could tell he was on the brink of being out of control. He followed her instructions, so she knew she could get through to him but only time would tell.

As soon as the call ended, Megan took out her earpiece. "We have a confirmation. He just told us who their target is. We were right. They are after the governor."

CHAPTER 26

Analysts from all over the state converged on the capital city. The anonymous call to law enforcement was receptive, but non-believing as well. They had to tighten the security around the Capitol due to a threat whether they thought it was credible or not. They were given just enough information. They had to prepare and in a big way. MoTAF knew nobody would believe an attack on the governor of Missouri, especially in or around his office. The clandestine operations to stop domestic terrorism needed to remain secret. The governor had a security force surrounding him at all times. The Capitol police had armed support from multiple agencies. The Jefferson City Police Department and the Cole County Sheriff's Department were on hand and making rounds in various locations in and around the Capitol. The State Highway Patrol, Troop F headquarters, and the administrative headquarters of the patrol's nine troop locations, were in Jefferson City. There would be police swarming the Capitol at every turn. If things were dire, the Missouri National Guard Headquarters was located only a few miles east.

MoTAF's analysts had a hard time believing young, twisted, misguided idealists, could pull off something of this magnitude. The plan, as simple as it was, would be almost impossible to pull off. It wasn't as if the governor's office was on a desolate highway in the middle of nowhere. They concluded there must be more to the plan and had to prepare for all possible variables. That was the only way to prevent a disaster. The threat had to be neutralized.

Analysts reviewed what was relayed to them about the assassination plot and reviewed it through its entirety. There were plenty of gaps in the plan, especially their escape. They had no escape plan that made any sense.

It was ludicrous to think it would work. It was too simple of a plan, or so it seemed. Brody was thorough in his recollection of what was going to take place. Their main concern was that it was simple, almost too simple. What they did not have was Ruben's part in the plan. He was the unknown variable. The very fact that his part of the plan was unknown made the plan viable.

A signature strike was warranted and granted. Whoever was acting upon any viable threat to the security of a public office would be eliminated. Those participating in the planning of, or attempting to facilitate heinous acts of violence, would be dealt with accordingly.

It was a normal morning at the state Capitol. Normal as any other weekday morning, except for one noticeable difference: police presence was obvious. Ruben noticed it right away, and it was hard for anyone near or around the Capitol not to notice. He was particularly happy he decided not to dress in drag attire. His tall, lean body would fool any man from a distance, particularly when he wore the long blonde wig he had acquired. Any up-close contact would reveal the obvious disguise.

He had done a cursory research of the legislative body that represented the county in which he lived. He was dressed in business casual attire. His nonprescription glasses would fool any person who looked at him cleaning the lenses, as if the newspaper he was holding under his arm required him to have them. If stopped and asked his reason for visiting the Capitol, he would inquire of the office location of state Representative Maddox. He had no intention of visiting that office. However, he had enough knowledge of small business investments in a town's local economy that he could talk politics with the best of them. Lawn service companies thrive when the economy is thriving.

Today would be a different day at the Capitol. He was already livid with the obvious intrusion of public privacy. Why were this many uniformed officers circling the Capitol and the adjoining downtown streets? The foot traffic inside the Capitol was even more nauseating. The Missouri State Capitol was an open Capitol, void of intrusions such as what he was witnessing. Anyone could walk into the halls of the historic masterpiece without being stopped by security personnel. Today, he wasn't so sure. There were different agencies representing a security presence not normally seen at the Capitol. Most were just standing and visiting with others as if it were a convention taking place in the Capitol rotunda. This was not the case. There were no speakers to be heard addressing those in arms. It had to be for one reason and one reason only. Ruben was convinced Lex, or the Kid had made a mistake. If either of them failed to carry out their respective task, it would be obvious who would be the recipient of his betrayal.

Lex had never felt as nervous as he did at this moment. He was sure he was going to be stopped by a sheriff's deputy as he pulled away from the Hampton Inn Hotel traveling on US 50 toward downtown. As the dome of the Capitol became the focal point of his drive and the view of his approach to downtown, he, too, noticed the obvious. Something was going on for there to be so much police presence in town. It unnerved him as he circled downtown. He had to be sure not to be seen by the same police officers too many times. He didn't want to stand out for any reason. He wasn't sure he could put the package he prepared in the sidewalk book deposit box in front of the library. There was no way he could not do it, but he did not want to explain using the sidewalk book deposit and not just walk inside the library to return the make-believe books. The deposit box looked like a mailbox, and he thought no one used the deposit box during the day. The metal box would not hold up to the explosion and would be ripped apart at the rivets. If anyone would be walking by at detonation, there would be collateral damage. The cost of patriotism had to be realized. The noon hour was fast approaching, and things had to stay on schedule. Timing was everything. He had to find a parking spot, deposit the bomb, and then head to the Capitol.

Brody didn't sleep much at all. He was looking at the clock in the hotel room, afraid he would miss his alarm. He knew not to ask for a wakeup call. That was one of the many demands from Ruben. Do not, under any circumstances, be remembered by anyone who may come later asking questions. Brody knew he was a marked man regardless of how things went. He just had to make sure Ruben was not the reason that things went badly for him. He had shown Ruben he could be trusted. He had shown everyone he could be trusted. That was one of the things that troubled him. He wasn't totally convinced he was not a scapegoat for anything that would occur. He was not sure though, that the so-called good guys could be trusted. That worried him, because neither he, nor Lex were aware of

Ruben's plan. Ruben was adamant about not concerning themselves with what he was doing or when he was doing it.

Brody found a location to park on the circle drive of the state Capitol. He had circled the Capitol twice without any luck. He became concerned by the number of parked police vehicles. They were everywhere. A state trooper was vacating his parking spot at just the right time he was pulling up to his location. He let the trooper pull out of his spot and smartly took it. If he had not, one of the other three cars behind him would have. A number of police vehicles were patrolling the streets as well. This all could not be good. How could this go down as planned with this much law enforcement at every turn. He could not focus on the obvious. He was not so sure Ruben was not the cause of them being there. He could have called in with some reason to get them converging on the Capitol as a part of his plan.

Brody looked at the time on his phone. He was in place and not a minute too soon. The foot traffic appeared normal, whatever normal was. Something was not right, and it made his gut turn. It was a good thing he had no breakfast. He was sure he would not sleep or have much of an appetite for weeks.

The backpacks he was given had his prints and DNA all over them. Could this be part of the larger picture in framing him with whatever was being planned? He was given the layout of the Capitol and knew exactly where to place the backpacks. Although Lex had scoped out all the locations, it was he who was doing the dirty work. It was hard for him to remain focused. He had never felt like this before. It was like a target was on his back, and he was just waiting for the impact of the bullet.

All three backpacks were black in color. They had different identification tags on each them. "KMIZ, ABC News channel 17;" "KOMU, NBC News channel 8;" and "KRCG, CBS News channel 13" were in bold colors and large print. They would not alarm anyone who would see them sitting anywhere unattended. It was obvious who they belonged to and less likely for someone to take them to a "lost and found" location. The nametags with phone numbers also gave credence to any onlooker. The padlocks on the zippers gave reason to believe they were for business. The assumption would be correct. The same networks unknowingly were assisting in the plan for breaking news, which they would soon be covering.

He wasn't sure he could place all three backpacks in their designated locations in such a short time frame. More importantly, how could he do it without being questioned or stopped by all the police? This was not a good situation he was put in. He knew, however, what he was carrying would not explode. At least, that was what he hoped. He was sure if the plan was going to work, it wouldn't be eliminating a key participant.

He powered up the extra burner phones Ruben gave him. He made sure each phone was on mute and placed one in each of the inner pockets of the backpacks. Enough shredded paper was added to each pack to make them look heavy. All he had to do was to deliver them where they were to go.

Brody's government phone chirped. He had been waiting for something from his unwanted, secret comrades--something to tell him they had prevented the threat to the governor, and everything could be called off. It was a simple text.

"We have eyes on you, Kid. Proceed as planned."

He began visualizing a big circle target on his back again, thinking he was not going to survive the day. He put a lanyard around his neck with false media credentials and walked at a steady pace. He entered the Capitol from the carriage drive that was open to pedestrians only. Maintenance vehicles were the only ones allowed that close to the Capitol entrances without proper identification and visual confirmation from security personnel. He made his way through the museum and found the stairwell. He slowly descended from the first floor to the garage basement level. He placed the backpack in the storage area at the bottom of the stairs. There were a few boxes and folding chairs cluttering the area. Nothing anyone would be alarmed about. The backpack lay on top of the boxes as if it belonged there.

He left the stairwell and walked the length of the basement parking garage. He saw the final resting place of their target and where he would be found after the carnage was over. It had to happen in the basement. There was no other viable solution to Ruben's plan. It was unnerving not knowing how he was going to pull it off, and what other despicable things he would be asked to do.

He continued past the meeting rooms and Capitol restaurant finding the west stairwell. More folding chairs were stacked in the storage area.

The placement of the backpack seemed too easy. His job was almost complete. He exited the west doors to the Capitol, circling around the south sidewalk back to his car. His nerves were easing. He could not believe how nonchalantly his mission was being carried out. He was greeted with smiles and "hellos" as he made his way through the Capitol. He noticed a parking meter chalk mark on the rear tire of his car as he approached. He had approximately two hours to complete his task before getting a ticket. He immediately cleared his mind of a parking ticket. He would be long gone before two hours were up. There would be no doubt that parking tickets would be low priority by day's end.

He retrieved the last backpack from his car and walked the same route he did his first trip inside. This time he walked past the visitor reception station and proceeded to the wall bench seats in the rotunda. He sat down at the end of one of the benches, placing the third backpack on the floor in plain view. He removed the cell from his cargo pants pocket and glanced at the screen. People were moving about but paying no attention to him. He was standing in the atrium of the rotunda, looking at the four balconies above. The architectural décor was a beautiful sight, which brought tourists from afar. The columns guarding the entry ways were picturesque of what was to come when entering. The Capitol's dome, topped with the statue of the Roman goddess of agriculture, could be seen from miles away. Today would be a day for tourists to remember--not for the bronze statues and fountains that surrounded the landscape for favorite photo op locations, but it would be as memorable as it was in Dallas, Texas, November 22, 1963.

Nobody was looking down at him from the railing above. He made one more glance around the rotunda before standing and walking away from the backpack. It was in place and not a minute too soon. He turned, glancing back at the placement of the backpack, just in time to see a man lean a camera tripod against the wall next to the backpack. It was Ruben. He could tell by his small stature and physique. He looked like a reporter as he was carrying a large video camera.

The elevator door opened, and Brody stepped in. He stared at the camera equipment and backpack as the elevator door closed. He had a smile on his face as the elevator started its descent to the basement floor. How perfect it looked. Ruben knew to complete the look for the abandoned backpack. Not even other media would question the equipment being there. His smile turned to a nervous blank stare as three police officers stood waiting for him when the doors to the elevator opened.

It was done; it was over. He was going to prison. He could not breathe in. He could not breathe out. He could hear his heartbeat and feel the pounding of his carotid artery. He stood for a brief second, frozen in place and stunned. All three moved to one side, allowing him to exit. He fully expected them to put him in handcuffs. As Brody stepped from the elevator, one officer smiled and nodded as all three stepped in before the door slowly closed.

He sat in his car with his head down, trying to stop his hands from shaking. The nausea feeling had returned at the thought of him being arrested. How did Ruben know Brody was going to be there at that very moment? Timing could not have been that precise, but it was obvious Ruben was watching him.

Lex had deposited his package and found a parking spot at the Capitol as planned. He was in place but was not so sure about everyone else. He was beginning to have doubts about the plan, especially when he had done the legwork for everyone. He knew the Kid had the same doubts. He could see it in his eyes when they verbally repeated their tasks to Ruben. There were gaps in the plan, and those gaps were Ruben.

The burner phones buzzed. Ruben sent both Lex and the Kid a text.

"Stay in place at the Capitol. I will let you know when to make the calls to the numbers you were given."

CHAPTER 27

Ruben started his short drive from the Capitol, east on US 54 to the Holts Summit exit. He never understood how you could be driving due north or south, and the highway signs would read east or west. He exited and crossed the overpass returning to the entrance ramp to westbound US 54. He immediately pulled to the shoulder where he could view traffic in his mirrors approaching the overpass. He glanced at the time on the dash of his car--12:38; the traffic was as expected. He did not have to wait long at all when he saw an approaching tractor-trailer. Things could not have worked out any better, as he noticed a panel truck following the tractor-trailer with traffic passing them both. He accelerated down the ramp just as the tractor-trailer merged to the passing lane allowing him to pull onto the highway. Things could not be smoother. Ruben wanted to extend an "Honorary Patriot Certificate" to the truck driver. Since when did a truck merge to allow entering traffic onto the highway? He maintained his speed slowing slightly to the same speed of the tractor-trailer. He was sure the other motorists were not happy not being able to pass the trucks. The panel truck remained in the driving lane. Ruben was now in the driving lane alongside the tractor truck. Other traffic was attempting to merge onto US 54 when Ruben increased his speed merging in front of the tractor truck on the approach to the third lane of the Missouri River bridge. Things were progressing quite smoothly. He pushed the button to open the rear cargo hatch. He then grabbed the rope with a knot tied at the end for grip. He gave a hard yank on the rope. The child car seat, with a life size doll, slid from the rear of his car to the pavement, at a three-car length distance in front of the tractor-trailer.

The truck driver had no choice but to avoid the child in the car seat as it landed squarely in the lane. Smoke careened from all the truck tires. The truck driver veered to the left causing the trailer to jackknife. Cars next to the tractor truck could also see the baby strapped in the car seat sliding on the pavement. The jackknifed trailer struck the two cars next to it, as all drivers attempted to avoid the inevitable. The panel truck had no place to go but into the rear of the car in front of him. The jackknifed trailer's cargo shifted, causing it to tip. The trailer disconnected from the tractor truck, careening on its side, blocking two lanes of traffic. All westbound lanes over the Missouri River were blocked.

Ruben exited the bridge and took the Capitol Street exit. As he turned toward the Capitol, he could see no traffic was moving across the bridge he had just traveled. Fire had erupted from the multi-car pileup. Eastbound traffic crossing the adjacent bridge slowed to a crawl as drivers witnessed the mayhem occurring.

Ruben pulled into the nearest state employee parking lot near the Capitol and drafted a text for Lex and the Kid. He unzipped the huge duffel bag in the front passenger seat and smirked, glancing at the outfit he was about to change into. He rolled his window down to listen for the first responders being called to the unfortunate traffic accident on the Missouri River bridge. Sirens began to wail from areas not far in the distance. Within a few short minutes, traffic was slowing on Capitol Avenue in the direction of the river bridge. No traffic was entering the city from the north. Before long, all traffic leaving the city would be at a snail's pace. He pressed "send" on his burner phone.

"Lex, in exactly five minutes, call the number I gave you. Kid, in exactly fifteen minutes, call the three numbers you have."

Lex and Brody were aware something was happening, and it was not from the text they had both received. Police cars in emergency mode, were traveling west around the circle drive away from the Capitol. Several officers were seen walking briskly, and others were seen running to their patrol cars. Once they got to their cars and pulled from parking locations, they activated emergency lights and sirens.

Lex watched his time closely, and the time had come. He dialed the number as instructed. He knew what was about to happen. Brody looked up as he heard a loud explosion. It echoed off the buildings where he was parked. He also knew it was happening. There was no turning back. Whatever got the police leaving the Capitol could not have been for what he just heard. He knew the bomb would cause damage to the book deposit box, but he did not realize it was large enough to make that loud of a sound. The concussion could be felt blocks away to where he was parked. It was the library. Brody wondered how could the device be so large as to cause damage to a place where young kids were likely to be? That would be heartless and unthinkable. Kids have nothing to do with the moral decay of state government. They should not have to pay for decisions of crazed sociopaths. Brody was becoming more and more sure of whose side he was on. He just had to prove it somehow.

Sirens were sounding from police cars traveling in different directions through downtown and around the Capitol. More police officers were leaving the Capitol, but this time all were jogging to their cars. The Capitol City was swarming with emergency vehicles; some marked by their respective agencies. Others were fire department volunteers who were called to wherever they were going. It was as if no one knew where the emergency was. EMS crews were responding but going in different directions. Ruben's plan was working.

Brody picked up his phone and started dialing. Surprisingly, the two reception desk employees at the entrance of the rotunda did not notice anything out of the ordinary, especially the putrid smoke aroma filling the upper floors of the circular rotunda. The smoke trailed upward in the rotunda as if being pulled by commercial exhaust fans. Not until a visitor from the museum came running to the desk did anything noteworthy seem to be occurring. The employees were in no hurry to investigate the excitement they were being told about. The gentleman told his female, co-worker to remain at the desk; and he would be back shortly. He followed the visitor, only to stop immediately when they came around the corner in the rotunda. The smoke was churning as in a funnel cloud circling up toward the Capitol dome. The backpack was about to be picked up by the employee when a loud popping sound could be heard, and flames started to emit from inside it. The museum visitor quickly walked away as if to go find others she may have come with to the Capitol.

The receptionist could see through the smoke and noticed the wood bench was becoming scorched and could easily catch fire along with the backpack. He ran to the desk and grabbed the fire extinguisher behind the reception desk. He knew he had to extinguish the fiery backpack before it got much worse. He ran to where he could see his co-worker at the desk and yelled for her to call the Capitol Police and notify them of a backpack on fire. She concluded the call and hung up the phone with the Capitol Police when two young teenage boys came running to the reception desk. They were frantically telling the attendant of smoke in a stairwell as they were attempting to take the stairs to the upper floor. They were excited enough to get the employee's attention for her to dial the Capitol Police again.

When the police answered the phone, the employee said "It's Beth again. I've got a report of a fire in the east stairwell. We need the fire department in the rotunda as well. Have them hurry!"

People were starting to gather around the reception area when someone came running to tell them again about a stairwell fire. The smoke was getting thick in the rotunda when it was then understood that the people talking about the fire in the stairwell were describing the west stairwell location. The reception desk called the Capitol Police once again and told them of a fire in the west stairwell and suggested they evacuate the Capitol.

In seconds, a loud siren could be heard throughout the Capitol. The receptionists started telling all who were standing around the desk to leave the Capitol and that the museum would be closing for the day. People were seen coming down the rotunda stairs as the Capitol offices started to empty. Simultaneous explosion sounds were heard at both ends of the Capitol. People started running for the exits, some falling as others tried to maneuver around them.

Two tall sheriff's deputies were directing people to the exits and trying to help those who had fallen. They were trying to slow down those who were running, all the while trying to keep others calm as they slammed through the south Capitol exit doors. A loud explosion was then heard, and people were fleeing from the blast that originated from the burning pile of cloth in the Capitol rotunda. People were no longer walking but frantically running from the Capitol at all exits. Nothing like this had ever been seen before.

The historic fire of 1911 had occurred from a lightning strike. The granite floor and walls would contain any current day fire of similar magnitude, or so it was believed. A fire was not exactly the plan Ruben wanted to set in motion, but it was serving the purpose of his master plan. Responding fire and rescue workers were obviously delayed. The traffic from all directions around the Capitol and the surrounding streets was at a near standstill. Sirens were blaring from police vehicles, but they were unable to navigate through stalled traffic. No one could yield to emergency vehicles because there was nowhere anyone could pull over to allow for them to pass.

Pedestrians started to fill the streets from the Capitol and surrounding businesses, as onlookers were taking in the sight of disbelief. People could be seen looking at their phones or making phone calls in an apparent attempt to find out what was taking place. A state of emergency was occurring in downtown Jefferson City! It was a scene from a science fiction movie. The only thing that would make this blockbuster complete would be aliens flying overhead in futuristic space crafts.

Ruben sent what he thought should be his last text. "Both of you wait for me at the 'fishbowl'. Kid, get inside with the one officer controlling the Capitol parking garage. You know what to do."

The fishbowl was the name of the circular police sub-station at the entrance to the parking garage. Lex learned the name of the sub-station when asking another tourist about directions in the city. He was told to go there, and officers would be able to help him. Lex never asked for directions but did learn the location of the office. It was small, round, and embossed with bullet-proof glass. The bollards were lowered from controls inside the circular office when owners of authorized vehicles approached. Those who could park inside were senators, representatives, other elected officials, and designated VIP's. The governor's vehicle was obviously one of the authorized vehicles. Bollards were lowered by the same officer when vehicles exited the garage. It was manned around the clock, seven days a week. Today was a useless endeavor. No cars were going in or leaving the parking garage. One impatient legislator walked away with the keys to the unattended car in the exit lane of the parking garage. Too many people were walking from the garage at the time somebody was wanting to drive out. The pedestrians did not care who he or she was, they were not allowing that car to move them out of their way. The garage was now blocked by one car. The governor was not leaving the Capitol, at least not by his security detail driving him out.

Lex and Brody easily found each other, even with their disguises, in the crowd. They were some of the visitors to the Capitol that day. Others were funneling their way out from the garage, explaining to each other the locations of their vehicles. They all realized they would soon be part of the city's traffic problem.

Lex and Brody realized quickly if anything was done to the officer, it would be witnessed by everyone. They spoke to each other stating the obvious and thought they were being set up.

"Why do you think all the police were here today?" Lex asked as they both looked at the crowds moving about.

"I'm sure Ruben thinks I called them," mentioned Brody.

"Or me," Lex said, glancing at Brody.

"If that's the case, we both could have a problem. A problem we can't afford."

"He's left us out of the execution." Lex looked around to see if anyone was close enough to hear him.

"Until now, I was thinking we were going to do it for him."

"With all these people around, I don't think so. That would be the death penalty."

Lex quickly responded, "For us, not for him."

Fire hoses were being carried from one fire truck that made it close enough around the circle drive to the Capitol. They were carried for connecting with the hydrant receptacles inside the Capitol. The cardboard boxes in the stairwells were on fire from the exploding backpacks. Fire in the rotunda was extinguished by several fire extinguishers that were brought from different locations on the first floor.

Ruben retrieved from the duffel bag his fireman's suit and put it on, as well as his helmet. Before entering the Capitol, he donned his full mask respirator. He was standing back observing what was happening around him. The smoke was thick where he was, and people were frantically making their way to the garage door. Most were coughing loudly as they were leaving. He stepped back from other firemen and joined others exiting. He entered the west Capitol entrance and saw firemen already attaching hoses to ground floor fire receptacles. He walked the length of the ground floor to the east basement garage door where he saw Lex and

Brody. He made his way to them, and they both turned away. They did not want to have a conversation with any firemen.

"It's me, guys. When the governor comes walking out with his security, Lex, you take out the lead two. I'll take the trailing two. Then I'll get the prize and will take him down. Kid, get into the guard office here and take out the cop. We don't want him coming to the aid of the governor. Fall in with all the other people walking, and you can come back and get your cars later. Meet up in the Truman Building dining area."

Lex and Brody said nothing until he disappeared into the smoke of the parking garage. "I didn't even know it was him," Lex commented to Brody.

"Me neither. Rather creepy I might add but extremely smart. Nobody knows what he looks like."

"We are fine. Our ball caps and sunglasses blend in with all the other tourists visiting today. We just happen to be at the Capitol. We're fine."

"People will look around when we make our hit," Brody said with concern.

"With all the commotion, nobody will notice until the security and the governor go down. We'll be gone by the time; anybody can come to help them."

Brody recalled the note he found in the sports page section of the newspaper. He had to be convincing when following the plan at the capitol. He knew he wasn't going to be the only one inside the fishbowl. He would be protected by MoTAF. He had to believe it. It was his only way out.

CHAPTER 28

Analysts on the fourth floor of the Jefferson Street office building had a bird's eye view from the rented, corner, conference room. The command center was perfect for real time operations. They could not see what was happening inside the Capitol, but they could see the security guard's office at the Capitol garage entrance and the entrance to the governor's mansion. The analysts in the room realized they had all players together for a split second. The tracer on Brody's phone linked with the data received from the multi-text sent to both phones at the same time. Ruben's phone could only receive an approximate location until the crash on the Missouri River bridge. They knew he was in traffic but not until the bridge was blocked and the cell tracking continued to move to the parking lot did they have Ruben's location. His tracking was lost again when he entered the Capitol. The analysts were all cheering when the tracking locator resurfaced on their screens again as the fireman exited the garage and joined with the other two at the fish bowl. No one had anticipated the smoked-filled Capitol. No one with MoTAF were close enough to risk entering the garage while not knowing which fireman to keep an eye on or to eliminate. They had to wait. They also were not equipped to deal with potential toxic fumes.

Chad looked at Megan and said, "Are you ready? it's time to go."

Without a response, Megan made sure her magazine was seated in her GLOCK.

"It's going to be warm with our vests on, but we've got to be careful. After you," added Brian as he opened the conference room door allowing Megan to exit.

Several analysts told them to be careful as they all left the conference room. They had help from all over the state. They received confirmation regarding who they were after, but no one was close enough to act when all three suspects stood together. They were all focused and were taking precautions, but no one could predict what was going to take place. They were very aware the assassination may not be prevented.

Chad, Brian, and Megan walked against the foot traffic as almost everyone else was leaving the Capitol. As they were approaching, Brian was pointing out other firm members and their locations.

"We have one inside the guard shack in the room below and out of sight. He's from our St. Louis Firm. We have two with us from the KC Firm."

"We have a lot of help today. I'd like to think they won't be needed," Megan said as they walked across Jefferson Street to the Capitol.

"Some you may recognize, but they may not acknowledge you," Chad said as he dodged people who were not giving way to their approaching. "As we planned earlier, you'll go in the fishbowl behind Brian."

"Be careful in the office. It'll be close quarters. I don't want anyone hit by friendly fire," replied Brian.

"But he's our inside guy, correct? We're not going to hurt him since he's helping us," Megan said in a concerning tone.

"We don't know what he'll do when he's surrounded. We have to plan for the worst," Chad said as he looked at her with a serious glance.

"I'll be fine. It's not like we're at Panera's. Besides, I came prepared this time."

As Megan walked up the sidewalk, she glanced at a lady coughing while sitting on a bench. She was looking at the lady as she looked up at Megan while continuing to cough.

"Oh my gosh, that was Shirley, my professor's administrative assistant!" Megan said to Brian and Chad.

"Yes, we know," Chad responded. "She's fine. Her coughing was acknowledging that she saw us and is in place. She's with us."

Megan wanted to turn around and look toward her but knew she should not. A man walked in front of Chad, also coughing, as he brushed up against him stepping in front of Megan. It was her professor. Megan couldn't believe what was happening.

"Stay focused, Megan," uttered Chad. "He was just saying 'hello'."

Their sunglasses covered who they were watching. Lex and Brody had moved to the front of the guard office near the entrance door. As they stood, Megan watched how Chad was looking at her and Brian while telling them the movements the suspected Patriots were making. He was smooth in his surveillance. Megan was not so sure they could prevent anything with the number of people loitering at the entrance to the parking garage. It was as if they all wanted to go back to work after the smoke cleared.

"They must have been signaled, and I missed it," Chad said. "A fireman came to the entrance and turned back walking into the garage. It had to be our guy. Notify command; it's going down."

Megan called the conference room command. They would alert all those on assignment that it was going down. Their cell phones chimed with the alert to engage the assailants at first opportunity. Without being prompted by the other, each MoTAF member tugged out the specially-designed badge that hung on a chained lanyard around their necks. Their suspected law enforcement identity would now be apparent to everyone as they mingled in the crowd. They also realized every one of them just put shiny, bronze targets on their chests.

Megan felt a nervous twinge in her gut. She had never been in a firefight before, and she was not planning on being in one now. Her dad had prepared her for the unknown, and she was confident in defending herself. She was not so confident about the unsuspecting people in the middle of the mayhem. She thought to herself about how all these people came to work to do what they were hired to do. Now, they were caught up in something they knew nothing about. Brian observed the two firemen coming to the garage entrance, then a third. They were waving their arms trying to get people to move away from the garage entrance.

Ruben stood with huddled firemen trying to extinguish the flames in the garage stairwell. He was watching the governor's vehicle. That is where he would come out. He could not get out of the garage riding in his plush comfortable ride; not this time. No cars could leave or enter until the abandoned cars were moved out of the way. Capitol workers were still streaming out into the hallways and finding exits from the building.

The governor's security detail got the incident assessment from the

Capitol Police. The Capitol's complex had to be evacuated. Fumes were filtering into the exhaust system and into the offices throughout the Capitol, including the governor's office. Firemen took a respirator for the governor to wear. The firemen warned all those who remained in the governor's office that the smoke and fumes would likely cause respiratory problems if inhaled. They all had to leave.

A fireman inserted his override key into the emergency key slot, which allowed the elevator to function. The elevator was exclusively used by the governor. You had to have a designated key to stop on the second floor, which opened deep inside the executive office. The elevator was small. The governor asked one of the firemen to allow one of his staff members to ride down to the garage. With that request, two staff members got on the elevator with four security officers and one firemen. The governor put on his respirator when the one and only fireman on the elevator keyed the controls. They started their descent.

Ruben heard another fireman telling others the governor was coming down his private elevator with a crewman. Ruben sent a text already drafted to Lex and Brody. He nonchalantly made his way to the elevator and waited for the governor. His right hand clutched the .380 automatic he had stuffed deep in the fireman's coat. When the doors opened, the fireman faced off with Ruben.

Ruben knew he could not take the shot at that moment. He would have to shoot the fireman and both staff members before he could get a shot at the governor. By then, at least one, if not two, of his security team members would get shots off at him. He stepped back, and the entourage started toward the parking garage. Ruben followed in behind trying to pick his moment. Both trailing detail members turned and watched him as they made their way to the garage door.

Lex and Brody were following orders. Brody tapped on the security door while showing his fake media credentials. The Capitol Police officer pushed the door ajar allowing Brody to step inside. Brody stepped inside the fishbowl and immediately noticed another person standing just out of sight and on the steps, that went down to the room below. He then got a push from behind, forcing him further inside. Brody turned around to see two people crowd in behind him. The one on the stairs now stood in front of him face to face.

The Capitol Police officer said, "Welcome. I think these people were expecting you."

Brody turned and looked toward the garage entrance for Lex. Lex turned to see if the Kid had neutralized their only threat. What he saw were two guys, one woman, and one officer standing around the Kid. They locked eyes, and Lex knew it was up to him and Ruben. He turned to walk into the long-tunneled parking garage when he saw them. Lex noticed two men watching him as he entered the garage. They were not exiting like all the other people. They were following him into the garage. They were hiding something in their right hands as they followed and watched him. They were closing in rapidly.

Lex saw the nicely-dressed men walking toward him all bunched together in a small group. Two were leading; two were behind. There were others, including a fireman, walking with a nicely dressed man in the middle. He recognized the governor. Lex was nonchalant, as if ice water was running through his veins. They did not know what was going to hit them. Lex knew he was made, but he had people and distance between them. He could not determine which fireman was Ruben, so he already had made up his mind not to shoot any of them. He had to shoot first and fast to take out security.

He drew his gun with his right hand and with a firm grip pointing the muzzle behind him and just under his left arm, between his ribs and his bicep. He knew the guy trailing him would have closed the gap and would be on him. Lex heard a guy yell, which he knew it was for him to stop. He kept walking, ignoring who was yelling at him. Lex felt a hand on his left shoulder. He pulled the trigger and the grip on his shoulder released at the same time he heard the man groan.

Megan saw one of their agents go down at the same time she heard the shot from inside the fishbowl. It was a large caliber handgun; people started running and yelling from the parking garage. Megan instinctively yelled at Brody to stay put and forced the door open, running to the garage. She drew her GLOCK when entering the garage, dodging people who were running toward her. Lex then heard a female voice shout from his unsuspecting left side.

"Gun!" yelled Shirley, as she saw Lex aim. She was close but not close enough to take her shot without hitting people running between her and the suspect, who just shot one of their own. There were people, including firemen, she was afraid of hitting even at this close range. She didn't know which fireman was the suspect.

Screaming people were now running toward the garage door exit. Brian was not going to watch any more agents go down if he could help it. He secured Brody in handcuffs with the aid of the other agent and the Capitol Police officer. Brian left the safe haven of bullet-proof glass and concrete, and entered the parking garage.

Lex did not see the woman shouting and looking at him but knew where the shout came from. He was aware his other threat was undoubtedly on him, so he turned to fire at whatever threat was coming. What he was aiming at were the backs of people running. Chad had moved to cover when one of their own had been shot. The Missouri State Capitol garage was turning into a war zone--a war Ruben and Lex were determined to win.

Lex emerged from behind a car engaging his main target. He could not see the governor, but he was on target and the protected shield would soon be down. The close-knit group surrounding the governor was running in a crouched position ducking behind parked cars. At the sound of the shots that rang out, the brunette next to the governor fell to the concrete with a scream. Another volley of shots rang out toward the governor, shattering glass of the sedan they ducked behind.

Chad engaged what he thought was the immediate threat. He knew he had to take him out and was determined to be the one to do it. Chad saw people falling, not all of them by accident. People were tripping over others who had fallen; others were falling from bullets that were not meant for them. He saw the shooter and knew he had to engage to stop the slaughter. He left his cover, aiming at the shooter. Chad could see the determined look of calm, but evil, on the assailant's face. It was cold, hard, callous and without remorse. Chad had him in his sight picture. His focus was precise, as he knew he had to end it. The shooter was exposed. Chad aimed center mass. His eyes were burning from the smoke. He squeezed the trigger as he was jolted at the waist almost knocking him off his feet. He did not see where they came from, but the two guys kept running with their heads down to the garage opening. Chad knew he missed. He also knew he shot an innocent bystander. She was turned from him but running to a hallway door leading from the garage back into the Capitol. Chad did not know if it was a ricochet or a direct hit. She fell face first into the door as the round left his gun. Chad instinctively turned to see the guys who ran into him escaping the garage. More shots rang out. People were falling as Lex kept aiming at the governor, but people kept crossing in front of him. His security team had grabbed the governor, holding him close while pulling him down and behind a parked car.

Lex lowered himself just in time as the rear glass of the car he was behind was shattered by several rounds. He knew he was targeted because he was the only one in the fight, so he thought. Ruben had not shown himself, and Lex was not sure he was still with him. Lex knew the Kid was compromised and thought Ruben was as well. Either that or he was left to finish what they both had started. Lex didn't remember or realize he wasn't hearing the shots from the suppressor on Ruben's handgun. He needed to get back on target with the governor. He was resolute to finish this.

Ruben reloaded and took the suppressor off his gun. He felt his precise aim, and misses were to be blamed on the makeshift suppressor device he put on the end of his barrel. He saw Lex still in the fight, now leaning behind a canvass top jeep. A poor shield if he ever saw one. It was time for him to come to his aid, and aid he would render. Ruben saw the security detail crouched behind a car. He thought he hit a trooper, as well as a fireman who was nearest the governor; but he could not be sure. He saw his confident Patriot handle himself in the fight. There was a lot of gun fire. He couldn't tell who was doing the shooting or even where it was coming from. There were a lot of them, but, where were they? There was too much smoke; too many people; too much screaming, running, and loud noise from large caliber handguns in the low, enclosed, concrete, parking garage.

Smoke and ammonia fumes were heavy in the garage. Lex could see the car the governor was hiding behind. The smoke was a shield for his cover as he made his way from one car to the next, getting closer to where the governor was. He was about to engage with the troopers surrounding the governor when a fireman who was hiding with them, stood up to run. The remaining male staff member, who was also crouched behind the parked cars, stood to run with the fireman.

A fireman hidden behind a car stood and fired several rounds, hitting the male staffer. The other fireman fell to the floor as well. Ruben realized the man running in the suit was not their intended target. He continued his assault.

Troopers, now crouched on top of the governor, were returning fire at an alarming rate. More glass shattered from where Ruben was hiding. He knew his cover was revealed, and his location was known. He was pinned down behind a car near the governor's vehicle. The troopers were relentless in their fight. Lex saw shattering glass of the car Ruben was hiding behind. Ruben had not left and was very much in the fight.

Brian now knew, as did all other players, who the shooters were. A fireman with a gun was no longer the unknown variable. Shirley had him in a cross fire and could eliminate one of the threats for good if it were not for that simple fact – crossfire. She would not go down from friendly fire and would not be the cause of the loss of a member of MoTAF because of her.

Lex quickly made his way to an abandoned car in the middle of the garage and walked in a crouched position, firing as he closed the gap on the woman who had identified him as a shooter. Lex heard a shot, felt pain in his left arm, and dropped his gun to the pavement. He didn't see who was firing at him as he ducked back behind a car. The woman continued to fire at him, and he felt rounds hit his right foot and ankle. Megan laid down on the floor of the garage, continued firing underneath a car, and engaged the threat made to Shirley. Lex drew his backup weapon from the small of his back, even though his pain was excruciating. Megan ran to Shirley's aid and cover.

Brian engaged the shooter who had lost one of his guns. He hoped he would attempt to retrieve it. When Ruben returned fire at the troopers, Lex limped his way to a jeep near Ruben's location. Everyone took cover again when shots were heard. No one could be sure where the shots were directed. The troopers were holding at their location. One trooper used his body covering the governor's, as they lay prone on the concrete. He was sacrificing himself to take any round before it would reach the governor. There would be no surrender.

Brian looked over to where Megan and Shirley had found cover. He saw three of the troopers looking for a target. It was understood, without question, they were not engaging the threat but remaining with their protectee. The governor was their responsibility; their only concern was for his safety. Megan saw Chad insert a new magazine in his gun.

Megan shouted over the noise, "Shirley, I think Chad's going in. He reloaded." They both instinctively did the same.

Chad glanced toward the governor's location and saw the troopers peering out from behind their cover. They were not going to risk moving the governor with a firefight in progress unless it was a last resort. Chad left his cover and, in a crouched position, started walking heel-to-toe toward the shooters. Megan and Shirley both left their cover and were doing the same. One trooper left his cover but remained at the rear of the vehicle where the governor was protected.

Chad started firing from his semi-auto in slow, deliberate bursts. Megan and Shirley followed in sequence. Two troopers were firing at the last location of the threat as well. The sound was deafening, echoing off the concrete acoustics. Ruben knew what was happening. From the sound of gun fire, they seemed to be circling him.

Even though glass fragments were falling on him and Lex, he was deliberate and calm. He reached in his fireman's coat and pulled out a flashbang, throwing it with all his might over the car, toward the shots that were being fired. The shooting stopped at the concussion of the explosion.

Lex left his cover and, without hesitation, limped in the direction of where the troopers had sought cover with the governor. As he got closer he picked up the gun he dropped. With his throbbing pain, he leveled both guns at shoulder height, pointing not aiming. The pain in his arm and leg made it impossible for him to hit any target. The troopers were holding their ears from the sound of the blast that was thrown in their direction.

Lex was firing both guns simultaneously. He was closing in on his target. He then made the mistake.

At the top of his lungs Lex started shouting, "Sovereign Citizen Patriots shall reign forever."

Megan was looking toward who was yelling. She balanced herself to her knees while leaning against a car she had crouched next to. Her ears were ringing from what sounded like a bomb. She immediately realized she had an advantage no one else in the garage had. The smoke and fumes were thick when she stood but not so much when kneeling. It was as if everyone had forgotten what they learned in grade school. When firemen came to show you their big red fire trucks and let you turn on the lights and sirens, they told you to crawl low below the smoke and heat to get out.

She was steady, using the car as support and holding the support grip on her GLOCK as her dad had taught her. She squeezed the trigger. She didn't have to question her aim. At this distance, she knew she would hit her mark. She was on target. Both rounds forced Lex's head to jerk to one side from impact. He fell without further movement.

Brian yelled, "Red Toyota. Fireman with the gun!"

Agents with MoTAF were fighting off smoke and fumes, as well as the ringing in their ears, but zeroed in on the red Toyota. What they did not know was two more firemen were now also hiding behind the same car. The sprinkler system in the garage finally started working. The shooting stopped but not for long. Ruben shouted for them to run, and the two firemen took his advice.

Both firemen heard Shirley yell, "freeze!" as other agents raised their guns at the two firemen. The security detail helped the governor to his feet. They didn't see Ruben raise his gun aimed at the governor. He fired at the moving targets as the agents returned fire. Ruben had to crouch down behind another car and started firing at feet from under the car he was behind. A trooper fell to the concrete floor, and Ruben knew the governor was exposed. He took careful aim as they were quickly moving to the exterior of the garage into the open air. A volley of shots was fired. The garage went deathly quiet, except for the sprinkler system that was now functioning.

Megan was still holding on her target, which was now lying on the Capitol garage floor. She could not remember how many times she fired. She just knew the threat had to be eliminated. She quickly scanned for any more threats, although she knew there were none. As she looked toward the garage door entrance, she could not see the governor or any of his security detail. She knew without a doubt Ruben had not been able to get any more shots off before she fired. It was like she had been instructed many times before on the range with her dad. Her sites were aligned, and she knew where her shots were going.

"Megan, Megan. Lower your weapon, it's over. Megan, lower your weapon," repeated Chad as he approached her.

It was as if she could not hear him. She was transfixed on her target still pointing her gun at the fireman lying on the concrete floor, a gun still in his hand. Chad kicked the gun from the lifeless body, reassuring her the fight was over. He walked to Megan as she lowered her GLOCK. She still had a two-hand support grip until Chad reached out. He touched her left hand gently with his; and she released her grip, lowering the gun to her side. As her hand lowered, Chad reached over and tenderly took hold of it.

"Are you okay? You had no choice. You did well," he said, reassuring her.

"Yes, I think I'm fine. The governor made it out." She continued holding his hand, but the grasp felt different as she adjusted her grip squeezing his for comfort while looking Chad in the eyes.

The Capitol Police officer in the fishbowl had called for backup support earlier when shots fired were first heard in the parking garage. Officers were finally starting to arrive as were EMS. Chad let go of her hand but smartly placed it on her waist as he stood next to her in an impromptu embrace.

Chad looked to Megan saying, "We've got to get Brody to witness protection. There's a lot to get done to clean up this mess. We can't be involved in any of it if MoTAF is to remain clandestine."

"Works for me, Mr. Jerguson, but how are you doing?" she asked with a smirk.

"I'm fine, Miss Swift, nice work here. I'm proud of how you responded in all of this." Chad motioned toward the carnage in the garage. "That was justice served on those guys."

"I agree. I would call it, 'Swift Justice,' ".Megan said as a large grin engulfed her face.

"Cute, Miss Swift. A comedian you're not. Once Brody is handed over, we should get over to the command for our prelim debrief."

"Let's do it. I hear they're having something catered for us to eat."

Chad looked at her and said, "Let me guess. Panera?"

Printed in the United States
by Baker & Taylor Publisher Services